SPIRIT
LEVEL

Sarah N. Harvey

ORCA BOOK PUBLISHERS

Library and Archives Canada Cataloguing in Publication

Harvey, Sarah N., author
Spirit level / Sarah N. Harvey.

Issued in print and electronic formats.
ISBN 978-1-4598-0816-4 (pbk.).—ISBN 978-1-4598-0817-1 (pdf).—
ISBN 978-1-4598-0818-8 (epub)

I. Title.
PS8615.A764S65 2016   jc813'.6   C2015-904474-X
C2015-904475-8

First published in the United States, 2016
Library of Congress Control Number: 2015946193

Summary: Harriet is a donor-conceived child who is connecting
with her half-siblings in this work of young adult fiction.

*Orca Book Publishers is dedicated to preserving the environment and has
printed this book on Forest Stewardship Council® certified paper.*

Orca Book Publishers gratefully acknowledges the support for its publishing
programs provided by the following agencies: the Government of Canada through the
Canada Book Fund and the Canada Council for the Arts, and the Province of British
Columbia through the BC Arts Council and the Book Publishing Tax Credit.

Cover and author photos by Shari Nakagawa

ORCA BOOK PUBLISHERS
www.orcabook.com

Printed and bound in Canada.

19   18   17   16   •   4   3   2   1

For Monique Polak
XO → ∞

ONE

"BE GENTLE WITH BONNIE," Verna says to me. "No rough stuff. She's had a bad week."

I nod and snap on the latex gloves. I don't always wear gloves, but to be honest, there's a big difference between massaging your own scalp and massaging the scalp of someone who clearly doesn't own a hairbrush and hasn't showered in weeks.

Bonnie eases herself into the chair in front of the sink with a sigh. She has left her enormous backpack—the kind you'd take on a two-month wilderness hike—beside one of the three chairs in the tiny salon. The filthy pack is festooned with grimy scarves, a couple of crocheted hats and what appears to be a collection of souvenir key chains—the Big Apple, Disneyland, the Eiffel Tower, London Bridge. Everything is attached with huge safety pins, like the ones you see on kilts. The pack is held together by a couple of bungee cords. A battered metal water bottle is stuffed into one of the side pockets.

"How you doin', hon?" Bonnie says to me as she leans her head back over the sink.

"Good," I say. "I'm good. How about you?" I test the water on my wrist. Too hot and the client screams. Too cold and they shiver. It doesn't help that one person's hot is another person's lukewarm.

Bonnie sighs again as the warm water reaches her scalp. "Glad it's summer. Easier when it's nice out."

I nod, as if I know what it's like to sleep in one of Seattle's many parks. I don't even like camping, which is kind of an obsession in the Pacific Northwest. And I'm pretty sure Bonnie doesn't have a tent or a nice Coleman stove or a home to go to if the weather is bad.

Damn. The water must be too hot, because Bonnie groans as it hits a spot near her left ear.

"I'm sorry," I say, but before I can adjust the temperature, she says, "It's okay, hon. Just a little altercation with a beer bottle."

I peer at a spot right above her ear and see a gash that should have had stitches. Another thing I'm sure Bonnie doesn't have is health insurance. The cut is healing, but it must be really sore. I work around it after I add the shampoo, but Bonnie still winces every now and again. Each time I say "I'm sorry," she says "It's okay, hon." I try to be gentle, and by the time I've finished shampooing, conditioning and massaging, Bonnie is snoring lightly.

As I wrap a towel around her head, careful not to rub the cut, she wakes up and smiles at me. One of her incisors is missing, but her teeth are otherwise in remarkably good shape. She winks at me. "Floss after every meal. That's my motto."

I help her into a chair in front of the mirror. "Thanks, Harry," my mom says. "I'll take it from here."

I spend the morning doing what I've done every Sunday morning since I was about twelve—shampooing, conditioning, massaging, getting clean towels, making coffee. I've also been in charge of the music since I got an iPod a few years back—every week a different playlist. This week it's Motown, and everyone sings along. Me, Mom, Verna, who owns the salon, and all the women who come for the best scalp massage in town, a free haircut and a cup of awesome coffee. Once in a while I sneak in some of the stuff I listen to, like Alt-J and Spoon, but most of the time the playlists are pretty mainstream. Classic rock, some country, Broadway show tunes. I actually like it all.

"*Stop in the name of love,*" Bonnie bellows, one grubby hand thrust out from under her cape, palm forward like a traffic cop. "*Think it o-o-ver.*"

Shanti, the woman in the next chair, who is younger (and cleaner) than Bonnie and dressed in a black micro-mini and a pink skank top over a lacy white bra, stands up suddenly and belts out, "*Haven't I been good to you? Haven't I been sweet and true?*" Everybody cracks up.

It's like this every Sunday at Verna's salon, which is called simply that: Verna's Salon. Not *Cut and Dried* or *Shear Madness* or *Mane Attraction*, thank god. My mom started working here when she was my age—seventeen. She says Verna saved her life. She was panhandling outside the salon and Verna took her in, fed her, paid her to sweep up hair and make coffee, gave her a place to live and taught her to cut hair.

Verna's eighty-two now and still running the salon. Lots of people think Verna and Mom are mother and daughter. They do kind of look alike: short, wiry, strong. They both have blue eyes and curly blond hair. Mom wears hers to her shoulders; Verna's is cut really short and is mostly gray now. I don't know what Verna saw in the kid sitting outside her shop all those years ago. I've asked her, but she never gives me the same answer twice. Once she told me it was because Mom looked like her dead sister. Another time she said she liked the fact that Mom was reading *The Bluest Eye* while she panhandled. Verna is a huge Toni Morrison fan. Maybe she just needed someone to help out in the shop that day. She was a widow, with no kids of her own. Never really wanted them, she claims. And then this hungry, angry, smart runaway turns up, and Verna takes one look at her and opens the door of her life. Just like that.

By the time I was born, when Mom was forty, she had a PhD and a good job, teaching sociology at a community college, but every Sunday we went to the salon and helped Verna look after her "Sunday ladies"—most of them women who couldn't afford the price of a good meal, let alone a shampoo, cut and blow-dry. The salon is my second home, and Verna is the only grandmother I've ever known. Ever since I can remember, I've loved the smell that clings to her pressed jeans and plaid shirts—peroxide, perm solution, hairspray, singed hair, the vanilla candles she burns to mask the other smells. A few years ago, she stopped doing perms and color. *Too many chemicals*, she said. But she still smells like the salon. Which is fine by me.

I started sweeping up hair when I was about five. No one asked me to do it; I just wanted a job, like everyone else, and I was a bit young to mix up hair dye or wield the scissors. *Here you go, Broomhilda*, Mom had said when she handed me a kid-sized red broom and dustpan. *Knock yourself out!* The Sunday ladies loved me. They brought me hard candies that I wasn't allowed to eat, and I hugged them and climbed into their laps while Mom cut their hair. When I was a bit bigger, Mom got me a stool and let me help her with the shampooing. To me they were just "Verna's Sunday friends," not drug addicts or drunks or prostitutes or bag ladies. I knew that Bonnie had been a chartered accountant until her drinking got the better of her.

And Shanti? She's a second-generation Sunday lady. Her mom was murdered by one of her johns a few years back. Shanti's real name is Rebecca, and she has three kids, all by different men. The oldest boy is autistic. When she first told me about him, I thought she said he was artistic (I couldn't hear her over the running water), so I said, *That's great. You must be really proud,* and she turned around and slapped me. Hard. Mom yanked her out of the chair and took her outside, hair dripping, and straightened it all out, but I'll never forget that slap. The sting. The sound. The way everyone in the salon froze. No one had ever hit me. Not even a swat on the bum. It made me wonder about Shanti's kids. Whether they had stopped being astonished at how an open hand feels on bare flesh.

Today Shanti (*It means peace,* she told me once) has brought her toddler, a little platinum-blond boy named Rocco, who spins himself around in the third chair while I wash Shanti's hair. When he flies off the chair, he doesn't cry. Maybe he knows better. He just shakes his head a couple of times and crawls up into Shanti's lap. I keep massaging Shanti's scalp ("Harder," she says) and listen to Bonnie, who is telling my mom about a guy with five hundred children. Which is impossible. Fifty, maybe. But five hundred?

"Was he, like, a crazy Mormon or something?" I ask.

"You mean a polygamist?" Mom says. "Not all Mormons are polygamous, you know."

"I know, professor," I reply. "I stand corrected." She frowns at me, but honestly, it's Sunday. Can't we skip the sociology lecture?

"How's your guy?" Shanti asks. "What's his name again?"

"Byron," Bonnie pipes up. "Like the poet. Mad, bad and dangerous to know. Right, Harry?"

"Right," I say. "He's definitely all those things." Although Byron is none of them.

I'm used to the Sunday ladies knowing about my life. They signed my cast when I broke my arm when I was seven and congratulated me when I won an essay contest last year. They've always taken a huge interest in my love life, such as it is. All the way from Trevor Miller in eighth grade (not good enough for me was the consensus, based on his failure to bring me flowers and chocolate on my birthday) to Byron, my latest. What they don't know is that Byron moved away two months ago—across the country to New York, where his dad got a job managing some big-deal dance company. He could have stayed in Seattle for his last year of high school—his parents gave him that option—but he chose New York over me, so I broke up with him. None of that "We'll Skype every day" shit. Long-distance relationships are doomed to failure. Everyone knows that.

But the worst of it is that Byron wasn't just my boyfriend; he was my best friend. It sounds like a cliché, but it's true. We met in kindergarten and bonded over the finger paints and our shared dislike of apple juice. And when our moms realized that we lived across the street from each other, they became best friends too.

So basically, Mom and I were both devastated when Byron and his family moved away. At first my friends called and texted, trying to get me to talk, to come out, to do something other than stay in my room and cry. I ignored them all, and eventually they stopped calling. Even my good friend Gwen gave up, and she's the most tenacious person I know, next to Mom. Gwen's gone for the summer now anyway, visiting her dad.

Mom catches my eye and says, "I'm ready for you, Shanti." She knows how much I miss Byron. She also knows I don't want to talk about it. Not with her. Not with anyone.

I pluck a sleepy Rocco from Shanti's lap and curl up with him on the old loveseat in the waiting area. I feel the way a lot of the Sunday ladies look: old and tired and ill-used. I put my head on the little pillow embroidered with the words *I am not afraid of storms, I am learning to sail my own ship*, close my eyes and let sleep bear me away. The last thing I hear is the ladies singing a fine rendition of "Respect."

When I wake up, Rocco is gone, the salon is empty, and my cheek is creased from lying on the pillow. One of Verna's afghans is draped over me. When Verna's not working in the salon, she's crocheting the colorful little squares that eventually become afghans. She makes at least six a year and gives them away to anyone who looks cold or in need of cheering up. Which is just about everybody in Seattle in the winter. Over the years she has tried to teach me how to crochet, but even she had to finally admit that all I was really good at was holding the skein of wool for her while she wound it into a ball.

My mom never learned to crochet either. Or knit or sew. She's not big on what she calls "the domestic arts," but she's been studying Tae Kwon Do since way before I was born. She has a black belt now and teaches classes for girls one night a week. I took classes for a while; I really liked the five tenets—courtesy, integrity, perseverance, self-control and indomitable spirit—especially after I learned to back them up with a really good elbow strike. That was the only move I mastered before a girl named Bethany Kirk almost broke my arm with a roundhouse kick, and I decided to quit. And yeah, I know you can get injured in any sport (I got a black eye playing basketball once), but with martial arts, you seem to be asking for it. It is kind of cool to know that your mom can beat the crap out of pretty much anyone though. Verna calls her "the titanium fist in the wooly mitten." And she's not just referring to physical strength.

I lie under the afghan and think about Byron. How far away he is. How lonely I am. On summer evenings when we were little, our moms would sit at our kitchen table, drinking wine and laughing or maybe crying (it was hard to tell sometimes), talking about whatever moms talk about. Work, men, kids, books, shoes, where to get the best bagels. Their voices were always in the air, like the scent of the honeysuckle that covered the fence. Mom would spread one of Verna's afghans on the lawn, and Byron and I would lie side by side in the backyard, waiting for the sun to set and the stars to come out. Usually we fell asleep before moonrise. The summer we were fourteen, he touched my cheek when he thought I was asleep. I swatted his hand away and said, *Do I have a bug on me?*

No, he replied. *No bug.*

A month later, he held my hand as the light faded. I didn't mind, even though I wondered why he was doing it. The next summer, when his arm grazed mine as he lay down next to me on the afghan, I turned to him and twined my legs with his. I hadn't planned it, hadn't noticed that my feelings for him were no longer entirely sisterly. How had I not realized that every-thing—and nothing—had changed? My lips hovered over his. I could smell the tuna casserole we'd had for dinner. I wished I had remembered to put on lip gloss and a nicer bra. When our mothers came outside later, calling our names, they found us breathless and slightly chafed. They looked at each other, grinned and shrugged. As if it had been their idea all along. The next day, my mom took me to the birth control clinic. While we were waiting to see the doctor, she said, *Good sex is about anticipation, Harry. That and respect, safety and communication. If you can't talk about sex, you shouldn't have it. There's no rush.*

I nodded and pretended to be enthralled by a year-old *Us Weekly*. When my name was called, I went in by myself while Mom signed some forms. I came out with a box of condoms and a prescription for birth control pills, which I never filled. Yeah, that's right; we decided to wait. It seems ridiculous now. All that time wasted being "mature," being "respectful," being "safe." I pull the afghan over my head and go back to sleep.

TWO

"I'M WORRIED ABOUT you, Harry," Verna says.

I stop sweeping and stare at the pile of hair on the cracked linoleum. It's late Tuesday afternoon. I slept most of yesterday, and I would still be in bed if Mom hadn't dragged me to Verna's. I have three jobs this summer. One is helping Verna at the salon, the second is dog walking (not my own dogs—Mom won't let me have one), and the third is being my mom's research assistant. I've been pretty useless at all but the dog walking so far.

I shrug and push the giant hairball into a corner. The effort makes me feel dizzy, which is ridiculous. It's a hairball, for god's sake, not a boulder. Verna is talking again, saying something about pulling myself together. I want to speak, but my mouth feels the way it did when I ate library paste in kindergarten—thick, sticky, slow.

"I'm okay," I mumble.

Verna takes the broom away from me and sits me down on the loveseat. "Clearly, you're not," she says. "You're heartsick. I can see that, but you can't sleep it off. Believe me, after Frank died, I tried. Didn't help. Every time I woke up, there was a split second when everything was fine—and then it hit me again."

I nod.

"So you know what I did?"

I shake my head.

"I worked. I kept busy. Real busy. I allowed myself ten minutes of crying a day. Then I went back to work."

Ten minutes a day? How could that be enough?

"Do you feel better or worse after you cry for hours in your room?" Verna asks.

I think about it and then say, "Worse."

Verna stands up and brushes some hair off her jeans. "Then there's your answer."

"My answer?"

"Life goes on, chickadee. Sooner you accept that, the better."

"Ten minutes, huh."

Verna pats my arm and says, "Start with fifteen. No more though."

I nod and straighten the pile of trashy magazines on the table in front of the loveseat, idly reading the headlines. The Kardashians are up to their usual tricks. I wonder what it would be like to have such a big family. Mom was an only child, and I'm an only child. I don't have a dad.

So no cousins, no big family reunions. No fighting with a big brother over the last piece of pie or yelling at a little sister for wearing my favorite shirt. I've never missed it.

My eyes fill again, but I don't want to cry in front of Verna, so I pick up another old magazine and read the story Bonnie was talking about on Sunday, the one about the guy with all the kids. Turns out he was a sperm donor who decided to contact as many of his kids as possible. All of a sudden I wonder if I'm one of them, which is ridiculous. Or is it?

I stuff the magazine into my bag.

"Do you need me anymore?" I ask Verna, who is counting the cash in the till and writing down totals with the stub of a pencil, which she licks every now and again.

She looks up at me and smiles. "Run along, honey," she says. "I'll close up here. See you tomorrow?"

I nod and give her a peck on the cheek before I head out.

When I get home, Mom is in the glassed-in porch she uses as an office. I stick my head in to say hi, and she gets up from the computer, stretches and says, "What's up? You're home early."

"Not much," I say. "Verna said she didn't need me."

"Lots of work here when you're ready," she says. "I've missed my assistant."

"Sorry," I say. "I'll get to it soon, I promise. Right now I need a shower." And a nap. But I don't say that out loud. Mom doesn't approve of naps.

She nods and sits back down at her desk. She's doing research for a book about homeless girls, and I'm her official transcriber. Better than any transcription software, she says, because humans can hear nuance. I listen to the recordings of the interviews she does and type them up for her. She's a terrible typist. She even has an old T-shirt that says *Never Let Them See You Type*. And yet she suggested I take Keyboarding at school. Not sure what changed (actually, I am sure—I've suffered through enough lectures about the three waves of feminism), but it's a useful skill these days. It's not like I'm aiming for a career as a secretary or anything. It's not 1962.

Anyway, the stories I transcribe for my mom are heartbreaking, especially since my mom was one of those girls, although she doesn't talk about it much. Who knows what would have happened to her if Verna hadn't taken her in? Now she's trying to, as she says, "give them a voice." She pays me fifteen bucks an hour to transcribe, and I had to sign a confidentiality agreement. I don't ask what good having a voice is if you're still hungry and cold and you ran away because your stepdad raped you and your mom doesn't give a shit. If I did ask, Mom would babble about empowerment and connection, about youth shelters and high school equivalency programs, but most of those girls will still be on the street. Not that my mom isn't sincere or committed—she is—but there's only so much she can do. She used to be a frontline youth worker, but she's a sociologist now, an academic.

The last interview I transcribed was with a fifteen-year-old girl named Angie (not her real name, of course; Mom gives them all fake names) who had been on the street for two years. When she was barely fourteen, she had a baby, who was immediately taken into foster care. Angie is a prostitute, probably an alcoholic but not yet a drug addict. She also has a genius-level IQ and a step-brother at Yale who is the baby's father. Her family has discarded her like a used tampon. It's a miracle she isn't suicidal. I would be.

I can't face anybody's misery but my own right now, so I go to my room and try to sleep. Sleep is the one thing I'm still good at. That and crying. But neither sleep nor tears will come. All I can think about is that guy and his five hundred kids. I grab the magazine out of my bag and read it more carefully. A phrase jumps out at me: *accidental incest*. Apparently, two of his kids met and ended up dating. It isn't clear whether *dating* is a euphemism for *screwing*, but either way, you know those kids are going to have hefty therapy bills and serious trust issues. A psychologist quoted in the article recommends that all donor kids carry around their donor's number and grill prospective partners before even going out for coffee. That would be one awkward conversation: *I really like you, but I want to make sure we're not related before I get in your pants.*

I'm not even *thinking* about another relationship and the whole idea of accidental incest freaks me out. Maybe I should find out about my half-sibs. How many, where, how old. It's not like I have anything else to do.

I get up and take a really long shower. Usually Mom yells at me when I shower for too long, but lately she hasn't banged on the door or pointed out to me that water is a precious resource. I kind of miss it.

I wash and condition my hair. I shave my legs. I can't even remember the last time I did that, which is gross, since it's been warm enough to wear shorts and a tank top for a while. The same shorts and tank top. I am down to my last clean bra. Definitely time to do some laundry. Mom hasn't done my laundry or made my lunches since I was ten. If I went to school in grubby clothes and had to eat crackers for lunch, that was my problem. I learned pretty fast how to measure detergent and make a decent sandwich.

When I get out of the shower, my head feels clearer than it has since Byron left. I'm excited about something for the first time in weeks. Maybe *excited* is stretching it; maybe *curious* is more accurate.

I suddenly feel shy—or more like wary—about telling Mom my plan, although that makes no sense at all. She told me years ago that she was a Single Mother by Choice (yes, it's a thing) and that I was donor conceived. I've known about the Donor Sibling Registry, a service that connects people with their half-siblings and/or donors, since before I could read. She's encouraged me to check it out and accepted that I've never wanted to. And now that I'm going to, I don't want her to know. I want this to be my thing, not hers. And it's not like she has any connection to my half-siblings anyway. She is not the common denominator—my donor is. (We never call him "dad," because he's not. Mom says "dad" is a social construct anyway, whatever that means.) All I know is that he was a tall, part-Latino medical student, which I guess accounts for my height, my dark wavy hair and my brown eyes. Mom knows a bit about his medical history, but I've never asked her about it. She always refers to him as Dr. GM (short for Genetic Material). When I failed Biology in tenth grade, she said, *Damn. I thought Dr. GM might have passed on some of those science genes.* Then she hired me a tutor.

Do I miss having a father? I've thought about that a lot. I know some great dads—I adore Byron's dad, even though he did drag Byron away to New York. My friend Anna's two gay dads have never missed one of her dance recitals, even though they're both big-deal lawyers. Martin has a stay-at-home dad who makes bread and coaches Martin's soccer team. But Brianna's dad fell in love with another man and moved to Detroit six years ago. He hasn't contacted her or paid child support since the day he left. Martha's dad is in jail for vehicular manslaughter. Gwen's dad left her mom two years ago and moved to France, where he lives with a woman who's not much older than Gwen.

So basically it's a crapshoot. Not having a father doesn't feel like an absence or even a lack. It's just a fact.

And really, can you miss what you've never known?
I don't think so. Dr. GM could be dead or in jail. Or
he could have raised three perfect kids who adore him.
He could even have grandchildren. It makes no real difference to me. It's not him I want to find. And I couldn't
even if I wanted to—you have to be eighteen to contact
your donor through the DSR. And they have to want to
be contacted.

Even so, I feel bad about excluding Mom from my
plans. Maybe I'll tell her later, when I've found one of
my half-sibs. Maybe not. I've kept some stuff from her
over the years. Dumb things like taking her car for an
unlicensed spin while she was out of town, or drinking
too many vodka coolers at a party (she probably figured
that one out—I was pretty sick the next day). And she
doesn't tell me everything either. I only know the basics
about her family: alcoholics, far away, not in touch, one
dead brother. She won't say why she never dates anyone
for more than about six months. And I don't ask. There's
a line you don't cross with my mom. If you do, you can
really see the tough teenage girl she used to be.

"You look better," she says when I go back downstairs.
"Less...snotty."

"Thanks, I think."

"Clean clothes too."

"It was time," I say.

"Past time," she says. "I'm about ready to quit for the
day. Shall we order Thai?"

I can't remember the last time I was hungry—I've been living on smoothies for a while—but suddenly I am ravenous. I call in the order—it's always the same—and set the table while we wait for the food to be delivered. One of Mom's weird rules is that we can only order takeout once a week (never more), and we have to eat it off proper dishes, sip our tea from small pottery cups, use place mats and wipe our greasy fingers on cloth napkins. So I put the kettle on and set out bowls and plates and red lacquered chopsticks (we both hate the nasty wooden ones that come with the food). I put a jug of cold water on the table and turn on the oven to warm some serving dishes. I even light a couple of candles.

"What's the occasion?" Mom asks.

"No occasion," I reply.

"Well, maybe I should be celebrating," she says.

"Celebrating what? The fact that I'm wearing clean clothes?"

She laughs and says, "No, but that too. You remember that girl I interviewed? Angie?"

I nod.

"She's off the streets. One of my colleagues was able to get her a spot in a school that's been set up specifically for street kids. She'll be starting in September. And she's living in a girls' shelter and working part-time at a grocery store. I thought you'd like to know."

Maybe I was wrong about having a voice. Maybe I've underestimated the power of sociologists. After all,

I'm named after one—Harriet Martineau, the first female sociologist. My mom worships her the way some women worship the Virgin Mary. Actually, I'm named after three Harriets. The other two are Harriet Tubman, the abolitionist, and Harriet the Spy, from the book. So far, I don't show any signs of being a sociologist, an activist or a detective.

I pour boiling water over loose green tea in a white teapot with a bamboo handle. "That's great, Mom," I say. "Nice to have a success story."

"So far so good," she says. "Lots of street kids can't cope with the structure of school or a job. They miss their street families more than they ever miss their biological ones. But we can hope for the best. Sometimes that's all we can do. And all victories, even the small or temporary ones, deserve to be celebrated."

"Sounds like you've done a lot," I say.

"Thanks," she says. "But the more I talk to these kids, the more I realize that you can never do enough, no matter how hard you try."

I think that's the saddest thing I've ever heard. Sadder than Byron leaving. Sadder than the polar ice cap melting. I can't bear it that my mom doesn't think she's doing enough.

"Verna did enough, didn't she? For you?" I ask.

She nods and rubs the little red grooves her reading glasses make on either side of her nose. She looks tired and worried, and I realize that it's not just about Angie.

It's about me too. The doorbell rings before she can answer, but I say, "I'm okay, Mom" to her retreating back.

After dinner I head to my room and go online to the Donor Sibling Registry. A long time ago, Mom paid for a lifetime membership with DSR. I could use the service or not, she said. My choice. She wrote the sign-in information on a pink recipe card, which she stuck to the refrigerator with a magnet that says *Be the exception, not the rule*. A lot of stuff has come and gone on that fridge over the years—drawings, cartoons, appointment cards, school photos, grocery lists—but the card was always there. Until now. Now it's sitting beside my laptop, a bit faded, kind of grubby. *Username: Dirtydog. Password: 1rainyday.* All the information Mom had about my donor is already entered on the site—donor birthday, donor ID number, donor type, name of facility, et cetera. It's up to me to make the information public. To check the little boxes and wait for a reply. It's optional whether you reveal where you live. I decide it can't hurt. According to the site, some people get a response almost immediately, and some people wait for years.

I consult the FAQs, read a few of the success stories, stare at the happy families in the photographs. Some of the stories are amazing—one woman found out that she and a close friend had used the same donor. Their kids were already good friends—now they know they are related! One person talked about being glad she had found her child's half-siblings in case anybody needed "a kidney or a lung or something" in the future. I'd never thought of that. It could come in handy, although it makes a sibling sound more like an insurance policy than a human being. But let's face it—if I needed a kidney, I'd probably be glad to have a few half-siblings to ask.

My cursor hovers over the little boxes underneath the question *Make Public?* I check them off one by one. *Click. Click. Click.* There's only one step left: adding a posting to the registry. The site says it's the most important thing of all. Once you do it, you open yourself up for what they call "mutual consent contact." Which sounds sexual but clearly isn't. I smile and reach for my phone to call Byron and ask him if he'd like some mutual consent contact. He'll laugh his weird, high-pitched cackle and then we'll talk about what I'm doing—whether it's a good idea or not, how many siblings I might have. He knows all about the sperm-donor stuff—and he's definitely not my half-brother. He looks exactly like his dad, who is Chinese, right down to a mole on the back of his left knee. I want to talk to him so badly I'm breaking a sweat. Then I remember. It's over. We decided. He's probably already dating one of the dancers in his dad's ballet company. The words on the screen blur, and I save my changes, set the timer on my phone for fifteen minutes, lie down on my bed and start to cry.

THREE

THE NEXT FEW days are torture. Limiting my crying to fifteen minutes a day frees me up to fret about whether to submit my posting on DSR. The possibility of hearing from hundreds of half-siblings—or none—freaks me out. I'm not sure which would be worse. I can imagine feeling either bereft or overwhelmed but nothing in between. I open my profile on the DSR site at least once a day, fully intending to take the next step, but I can't make myself do it. I go to the salon for a few hours every morning, and I take the dogs out for a walk in the afternoons. Most of the dogs are rescues—a little brown mutt with a huge personality, two adorable beagles, a gigantic German shepherd-rottweiler cross who is the sweetest dog on the planet. And maybe the strongest. Thank god she's well trained. They all get along really well, but even their antics don't stop me pining for Byron or worrying about the donor thing.

I've started working for Mom again too, although I'm finding it really hard to concentrate. Sometimes it takes me ten minutes to transcribe a single sentence. Sometimes I read back what I've transcribed and it makes no sense at all, as if I had only heard every third word.

I finally submit my DSR posting on Sunday after dinner. Mom is at the youth shelter where she volunteers and does her interviews. I've had a good day—one of my favorite clients, a girl my age named Annabeth, showed up at the salon. She's been coming in for a couple of years, and she volunteered to be interviewed for Mom's book. When I typed up her transcript, I knew it was her, even though Mom gave her a fake name. Mom read me the riot act about respecting Annabeth's privacy. I was never to discuss anything I learned from any of the transcripts with anyone, but I was to be especially mindful (Mom's word) when I saw Annabeth at the salon. Annabeth knows I'm Mom's transcriber, but she doesn't seem to mind that I know a lot about her life. She even jokes about it sometimes, although there's not much to joke about. She's blind in one eye because her mom beat her when she was a baby, and she's been in and out of foster care most of her life. She prefers life on the streets to having a permanent roof over her head. Most of the homes she has been in were, as she puts it, shitholes run by assholes.

She makes money singing on street corners. Old jazz standards—"Summertime," "All of Me," "Blue Skies." She doesn't do drugs or drink.

She hasn't been to school since sixth grade, but she spends part of each day in the library, where she can't get a library card because she doesn't have an address. She reads biographies of singers—Ella Fitzgerald, Billie Holiday, Aretha Franklin, Etta James—and then listens to YouTube clips on the library computers. Her prized possession is a set of cheap earbuds. Her dream is to go to a performing-arts school.

There's something about Annabeth—the way she chooses her words, the lilt in her voice, her calm acceptance that life is a nightmare, her joy when she sings along to my playlists—that makes me want to bring her home, feed her, share my bedroom with her, lend her my clothes, pay for singing lessons, enroll her in a school that has a music program.

Mom says the best I can do is pamper her on Sundays. "Boundaries," she reminds me.

"Bullshit," I say. "Verna took you in."

"That was different," she says. End of discussion.

So I haven't done anything yet other than give Annabeth a scarf I knit last winter. And lend her books. We always talk about books—we both love *To Kill a Mockingbird* and hate supernatural/paranormal romance.

Today, though, as I wash her hair, she says, "I met a guy who said he'd get me a record deal."

"That's awesome!"

"I think he might be a pimp though."

"Really?"

"He offered to set me up in an apartment. What does that sound like to you?"

My experience of pimps is limited, but Shanti would know. She's not at the salon today, but I'm sure she'll be in soon. "What's his name? What does he look like?" I ask.

"White, skinny, mid-forties. Little mustache. Nice clothes. Drives a white Beamer. He says his name is Brad."

"I'll ask around," I say. She closes her eyes as I massage her scalp, and we both hum along to "Someone to Watch Over Me." For the hour that she's in the salon, I can be that someone for her.

Three long days later, I get my first communication through DSR.

Subject line: Hello, Harriet

I stare at the words for such a long time that they start to blur. Then I click on the message to open it and squeeze my eyes shut as the words appear on the screen. What if there's a photo? What if I don't like him/her? Or he/she doesn't like me? What if he/she's stupid or mean or super right-wing? What if he/she doesn't like reading? What if he/she only listens to Christian country music? What if—

I squint with my left eye. The message is still blurry, but there's no photo. I open both eyes and read the message.

Dear Harriet,

My name is James Miller. I live in Sarasota, Florida, with my mother, stepfather and two sisters. We moved here from Arizona when I was five. I am twenty-one years old and have been searching for my half-siblings for a year now, with very little success. Genealogy has been a particular interest of mine since our family joined the Mormon Church when I was fifteen. I would love to get to know you and talk to you about my faith. I recently returned from a mission in Argentina, where I was able to lead many into the fold.

Yours truly,

James Miller

This is even worse than I imagined. No way do I want to end up on some Mormon's ancestral roll. I delete the message immediately, my hand shaking. Then I feel bad for James Miller; he's obviously not what Mom would call "socially adept." I mean, who starts a relationship with proselytizing? Maybe he's a great guy, religious beliefs aside. Or maybe this has all been a huge mistake. I'll give it another week and then take my post off DSR.

No harm, no foul. In the meantime, I retrieve James's email from the trash and put it in a folder labeled *Donations*.

Then another email arrives. Not from James, thank god or Moroni or whoever it is Mormons worship.

Subject line: SISTERS!!!!

Hi, Harriet,

My name is Lucy Tanaka. Sorry about all those caps and !!! I'm pretty excited, especially since we both live in Seattle. I'm 15 and I live in Wallingford. I have an older half-brother named Adam. He's 20 and lives in Oregon, where he goes to college. Same donor, different mother, so he's your half-brother too. I told him I was doing this. He says hi. No exclamation point or caps. But that's just Adam. In case you haven't figured it out, Adam and I have two moms, Nori (my mom) and Angela (his). They both know I'm looking for my sibs. I really want to meet you. Where do you live? So stoked!!!!

Your sis,

Lucy

PS I love your name.

PPS I found another half-brother a while ago on DSR. His name is Ben—he's 22. He lives in Australia.

Holy shit! Not only do I have a half-sister, but she's here. Practically around the corner. I can actually meet her, which is kind of scary but also pretty exciting. Even though the DSR advises exploring new sibling relationships slowly,

I can't see the advantage of dragging it out. Email is a shitty way to get to know a person. Before I can think better of it, I type a reply and hit *Send*.

Hi, Lucy,
Thank you for writing. Yes, I would like to meet. I live in Victory Heights. Maybe we could meet in the U District on Monday afternoon around 3? You choose a place.
Harriet Jacobs

Less than a minute later, the computer pings with her reply.

Yes!!! Meet me at Café Allegro. I love that place! They have the best chai lattes. Can't wait to see you.
XXXOOO Lucy

I close the computer and sit back, my heart racing. How could it be this easy? This straightforward? Lucy's emails sound so...normal. Not all angst-ridden. Sort of... sunny. Monday is five days away, and all of a sudden I can't wait to meet her. My little sister. I email her back and say: How about Saturday instead? Same time and place? How will we recognize each other?

What I don't say is that if I have to wait until Monday, I'll drive myself insane with worry and probably confess everything to Mom. I don't want to do either of those things.

Sure, she writes back. Saturday is awesome. I'll be there—with bells on. In case you hadn't guessed, I'm half Japanese.

I'm tempted to write back and attach a photo of myself, but I decide not to. It's not much to go on—there are tons of teenage Japanese-American girls in Seattle—but maybe it's better this way. Less clinical, more spontaneous. Lighthearted, almost, like Lucy's emails. Not a big deal at all.

To try to distract myself while I wait, I transcribe an interview for Mom. This one is with a sixteen-year-old girl named Mattie who has been homeless for six months. Her mother is a violent alcoholic. Her brother is a convicted murderer. Her father is long gone. Her sister died from an overdose when she was eighteen. Mattie panhandles and deals a bit of weed, although she says she hates drugs. She is almost illiterate. The only thing she has in the world is her dog, Leroy, a pit bull cross that she rescued from a Dumpster when he was a newborn. Leroy will attack anyone who lays a hand on her, but she can't take him into a shelter. They sleep in parks or in shop doorways or occasionally on someone's couch. She always feeds Leroy first. Sometimes she ties him up outside the library while she goes inside to try and clean up. Her biggest fear is that Animal Control will take Leroy away from her because he has no dog license. When Mom asks her what would make her life better, she says she'd like to find a shelter that will allow dogs and she'd like to take Leroy to the vet, because he's been limping lately.

And I'm freaking out about meeting my half-sister in a coffee shop.

I stress about what to wear to meet Lucy. Shorts and a tank top seem too casual. My favorite skirt has a blob of dried yogurt on it. My favorite capris are wrinkled. I finally settle on a cute blue halter dress I found in a vintage shop last spring. I put on my red wedge sandals, twist my hair up in a loose bun and walk to the bus stop.

I get to the coffee shop early and lurk at a back table, thumbing through a foodie magazine someone has left behind. Reading recipes usually calms me down. All those precise measurements and logical steps. Everything in its proper place. I'm not much of a cook, but I do like baking. A recipe for bacon brownies diverts me briefly—disgusting or delicious?—but soon I'm back to worrying about meeting Lucy. She's only fifteen, for god's sake. What's there to be worried about? Worst-case scenario, we meet, have a chai latte, discover we have nothing to say to each other and go our separate ways. Best-case scenario—well, I can't even imagine what that would be. Having a sibling is a mystery to me.

I'm keeping an eye on the front door, and when she comes in there's no doubt in my mind that it's her, even though she looks like a twelve-year-old. She's tiny—probably not even five feet tall—with black hair in a long ponytail. She's wearing a turquoise T-shirt and cargo shorts with huge pockets. She's also ringing a tiny bell—as if she's leading a meditation group. (Mom had a meditation phase; the bells drove me crazy.) To be accurate, she is actually striking two teensy cymbals together. She wasn't kidding when she said she'd be here with bells on. I also know it's her because someone in the back of the café calls out, "Hey, Lucy!" and she yells back, "Hey, Nate." For such a little person, she has a surprisingly big voice.

I stand up and lift a hand in welcome, feeling huge and clumsy. She sees me and darts toward me, cymbals tinkling, a huge grin on her face. Her teeth are very straight and very white. Orthodontics or good genes? I had braces for years, so I'd guess orthodontics. And some White Strips.

She stops right in front of me and says, "You look just like him! I would have recognized you anywhere! Hug?"

Without waiting for an answer, she throws her arms around me. She's seriously strong. I end up patting her on the back.

"Who do I look like?" I ask when she finally steps back and jams the cymbals into the outside pocket of her khaki messenger bag.

"Adam. My brother. Your brother. Nori's Japanese. Angela isn't." She digs in her bag and pulls out her phone.

"Look," she says. "This is Adam. Brown eyes, wavy dark hair, olive skin, tall. Just like you."

I look at the phone. She's right. I do look like him. A lot. She turns the phone on me, takes my picture and says, "Can I send it to him? Please? It's gonna blow him away. How much you look like each other."

I nod dumbly as her thumbs fly over the phone and the message swooshes away. Everything is happening too fast. I need to sit down, take it all in. Digest it. I start to lower myself into my chair, but Hurricane Lucy is already on the move.

"You want a coffee? Or some tea? They have great tea here. Nori says I shouldn't drink so much coffee."

She grabs my hand and pulls me over to the counter, where I order a mocha and a blueberry scone, and she gets a chai latte and a cinnamon bun. "With extra icing, Nate," she says to the cute guy in the plaid shirt who takes our order.

"You got it, Luce," he says.

"Do you come here a lot?" I ask while we wait for our drinks and food.

"Three or four times a week since I was, like, ten," she says. "My dance studio's just around the corner. On Saturdays I'm there all day—teaching Baby Ballet and taking classes. I get soooo hungry. Nori always wants me to pack a 'healthy lunch'"—she puts the words in air quotes—"but the food's awesome here, and they take care of me. I'm kind of like the café mascot."

As if on cue, Nate brings our order to the table and hovers around for a few minutes, asking us if we've got everything we need, how we know each other and whether I live nearby. I tell him everything looks great and don't answer his other questions. When he finally leaves, Lucy leans across the table and whispers, "He was totally flirting with you!"

I glance over at him—he's behind the counter making coffee, but he looks up and catches my eye and smiles. I blush and look down at my scone.

"He's a friend of Adam's," Lucy says. "So it wouldn't be like a blind date or anything."

"I have a boyfriend," I say stiffly.

"Oops," Lucy says. "My bad. Nori says I'm, like, addicted to matchmaking. And you gotta admit—he is hot."

I take a sip of my mocha. I don't know why I lied to Lucy about having a boyfriend. Not a great start. Almost as bad as proselytizing. I'm no better than our Mormon brother.

"So you've been dancing a long time?" I say.

"Forever. I love it. Nori started me in Baby Ballet when I was two. I was kinda hyper and she thought it might, you know, chill me out."

"Did it work?" I ask.

She laughs—loudly—and says, "Nope, not really, but it kept me busy. Still does." She takes a big bite of her cinnamon bun, following it with a gulp of her latte, and says, "What's your thing?"

"My thing?"

"You know. Your passion. Your obsession."

I'm saved from answering by the return of Nate, who wants to know if we need anything else. I ask him if he can bring me some more whipped cream for my mocha. I don't even like whipped cream. Then I ask where the washrooms are and excuse myself from the table. Anything rather than answer Lucy's question.

What should I say? That I give an excellent scalp massage? That I'm a fast typist? That I write a great essay? That I like reading and listening to indie bands? No way am I going to tell her that I don't really have a "thing." When I come back from the washroom, Lucy is texting again.

"Adam says it's scary. How much you two look alike."

I nod. I'm not sure *scary* is the right word, but I know what he means.

"And I sent Ben your picture too."

I can't help it. I frown at her and say, "Why did you do that?"

She puts down her phone and says, "I'm sorry, Harry. I should have asked first. Adam says I always come on too strong."

I shrug. "It's a weird situation, for sure. Hard to know where to start."

"I'm sorry," she says again, and I can see that she is trying not to cry.

"It's okay. Really." I reach out and touch her hand.

"I'm such an idiot," she mumbles. "I've been wanting a sister for sooooo long and now you probably hate me."

I hand her a napkin and say, "I don't hate you. I'm just not very good at talking about myself, I guess. And I don't have a boyfriend. He moved to New York, and we broke up. I'm sorry I lied to you."

"You broke up? Why?"

"'Cause New York is so far away and Skype is so lame."

"But...don't you love him?"

"Yeah, but we'd never be able to see each other. So I decided to rip off the Band-Aid, go cold turkey."

The look of horror on her face is almost comical. You'd think I'd just told her that I only had three weeks to live. "Are you always like this?" she asks.

"Like what?"

"So..." She stops and blows her nose on the napkin. "So sensible."

For the first time all day, I laugh. I'm not sure why. It's not exactly a compliment to be called sensible, but it's hardly an insult either.

"Yeah," I say. "I guess I am. But you know what? Maybe it's time I stopped." I pick up my mocha and drain it in one gulp. I can almost feel the sugar rushing through my veins. "Maybe I should ask Nate out."

"Seriously?"

I shake my head. "Not really. Too soon. But he is cute."

Lucy nods. "He's only working here until he gets his big break as an actor. A while ago he was Stanley in *Streetcar*.

He was all broody and gross for weeks. One review called him 'promising' but another said he was 'a limp hipster imitation of Brando.'"

"So he'll be here a while," I say. "If I decide I need a broody actor boyfriend."

Lucy cracks up. "I'm sorry I called you sensible," she says as we head out of the coffee shop. "And I'm sorry I sent your picture to Ben without asking first. And I'm sorry I have to go back to the studio for my pointe class."

"It's okay," I say. "Really. I'm not upset. And I'm glad you sent Adam and Ben my picture. Maybe you could send me theirs too—so we're even."

She nods vigorously and hugs me again before we go our separate ways. "Promise we'll get together soon? Maybe you could come and watch me dance. Or you could come to my house and meet Nori and Angela. We could Skype with Ben."

"I promise," I say. "Don't worry. You haven't scared me off. Not yet anyway."

Her face starts to crumple—she looks like a toddler whose balloon has drifted away—and I add, "Just kidding."

She slings her messenger bag across her body and says, "Gotta go. Bye, big sis. Call me." She takes off down the street, the bag bumping against her hip, and I wonder if this is what being a big sister feels like: protective, annoyed, amused and confused.

FOUR

LUCY TEXTS ME an average of four times a day for the next couple of days until I agree to meet her on Tuesday at the same coffee shop. Clearly she's on "full steam ahead" while I'm on "proceed with caution," but she doesn't seem to notice. Eventually she wears me down with her emoticons and her general chirpiness. Today she is wearing cutoff jeans and an embroidered peasant blouse; her hair falls in a shiny black cloak to her waist. On one arm are about fifty sparkly metal bangles that chatter and clank as she waves her arms and talks. Her fingernails are bright orange. I feel drab and lumpy in my (now clean) dark denim skirt and green T-shirt, with my hair pulled back in a messy ponytail.

Over our drinks, Lucy tells me her favorite color (turquoise, but also tangerine, hence the nail polish), why she's afraid of small dogs (bitten in the face by a

Chihuahua when she was a baby—see, she still has a tiny scar), how much her dance school costs per month (a lot!), what she thinks about gay marriage (totally for it, obviously; she wants to plan Nori and Angela's wedding, but they want something simple, which is so boring), how many pairs of pointe shoes she has worn out (hundreds!), how strong ballet boys have to be and how they aren't all gay (especially Paul, whom she has a crush on but he's way too old for her). She loves rare steak, dill pickles and lemon meringue pie. She watches old Disney movies when she's tired or sad.

I'm about to tell her about Verna and the Sunday ladies when she says, "Oh, I forgot. Nori and Angela want you to come for dinner soon. Your mom too."

"My mom doesn't know about you yet," I say.

A tiny furrow forms between Lucy's perfect eyebrows. I wonder whether she gets them done professionally or if they just grow that way. I run a finger over my own brows, which feel bushy and unkempt.

"Why not?" she asks. "Are you ashamed of me or something?"

"Ashamed? Of course not. I just haven't told her about looking for my sibs. I was planning on telling her."

"When?"

I shrug. "Soon, I guess."

"You always this secretive?" Lucy licks her finger and picks up muffin crumbs from her plate.

I shrug again. "Not really. I've never really had anything to be secretive about. Mom's big on communication, as long as she's not the one doing it. She's always saying, *You can tell me anything.* Usually I do. Just not this time."

"Angela's like that too, but Nori says that sometimes I overshare. Do you think that's true?"

I think about some of the other stuff Lucy has told me. For example, Nori grew up in San Diego and married her high school sweetheart, a guy named Howard, who developed a serious Internet porn addiction. She divorced him and ended up living on a collective farm in northern California, where she met Angela. They fell in love and moved to Seattle, where Angela trained to be a midwife and Nori became a garden designer. Angela actually delivered Lucy, at home, while Adam watched. Adam and Angela don't get along, which is why he moved away to go to college, where he is studying business. Maybe he never got over the trauma of watching his little sister's birth.

"I don't know," I say. "I mean, we just met. It's hard to know what to say, what to leave out."

She frowns again. "Why is that so hard? We're sisters. We should tell each other everything, right?"

She sounds so much like a bossy ten-year-old that I have to laugh. After all, what do I know about being a sister? Maybe she's right. It's just that my "everything" is so much duller than hers.

"Maybe not everything," I say.

"But you will tell your mom?"

"Yeah. Soon."

I get up to grab some hot water for my tea, and when I come back to the table, she's having an intense FaceTime conversation with someone.

"She's right here," Lucy says to whoever's on the phone. "Hang on a sec." She holds the phone out to me. "It's Ben. In Australia. Wanna say hi?"

I don't see how I can say no, although I want to. I hate having things sprung on me—Verna calls it being "wrong-footed"—but Lucy doesn't know that yet. I take the phone and smile at it and say, "Hi, Ben." Ben smiles back. He doesn't look at all like me or Lucy. He's got short blond hair and bright blue eyes. He looks like a surf bum.

"Hi, Harriet." He yawns, and I can almost see his tonsils. He has no fillings. Neither do I. Good genes, I guess. "Nice to meet you."

"What time is it there?" I ask.

"Early. Lucy never gets the time difference right."

"I do so," Lucy yelps. "You're just lazy. It's morning there."

"And I worked until two," he says.

"Oops!" Lucy giggles. "Sorry, Ben."

"What do you do?" I ask.

"Bartender. While I'm in school." Ben yawns again. "Trying to keep the debt load down."

"He's gonna be a famous architect," Lucy says.

"Cool," I say. My conversational skills, such as they are, seem to have vanished. He must think I'm an idiot. "Look, I should run," I say. "Late for work myself. Bye, Ben." I hand the phone to Lucy, but not before I see the look of surprise on Ben's face. I'm disappointing everyone today. Lucy says goodbye to Ben and puts her phone away.

"That was rude, Harry," she says. "Super rude. Ben's a good guy. And he's your brother. I'm going to class." She grabs her messenger bag and flounces out of the café. Really, that's the only word for it. I consider going after her, but I don't have the energy. So far, I'm not very good at the sister thing.

I don't hear from Lucy for a few days, and I'm about to text her and apologize when I get an email from another half-sister.

My name is Meredith Leatherby, and I found you on DSR. I guess we're sisters. Half-sisters. I'm from Montana originally. Moved to Seattle a while ago. Since our donor used a Seattle facility, I was hoping to find some of my siblings here. Are you available for coffee sometime?

No "Dear Harriet," no "Cheers." Not even a "Yours truly." It's not the warmest email I've ever received, and I wonder if she's found Lucy through DSR too.

Instead of writing back to Meredith, I pick up my phone and text Lucy.

Sorry I was rude to Ben. I'd like to call him to apologize. I just got an email from a girl called Meredith. Another sister. She wants to meet. You up for that? If so, when? I miss you.

I send the text before I can delete the last sentence, then reread Meredith's email. It still sounds cold. Or maybe she's just really reserved. Compared to Lucy, everyone seems reserved. And dull. Including me.

I start working on another transcript for Mom while I wait to hear from Lucy. Unlike most of the girls Mom interviews, Sonia comes from a middle-class family that she calls *totally white bread. My parents are rich and boring as fuck. My dad's a lawyer, my mom's a doctor. How cliché is that?* She is their only child, raised in Ann Arbor, Michigan; she first ran away when she was thirteen. Why? She wasn't abused—in fact, she was well loved. She admits that. But she was bored. Or, as she puts it, *supremely, mind-numbingly, soul-destroyingly bored.* Every time she got caught, she'd wait a while and then run again. Over and over and over. Thousands of dollars wasted on therapists, none of whom believed that she was simply bored out of her mind, even though she never stopped telling them. Special schools, acting classes, an expensive guitar, a trip to Paris. None of it interested her. The family cat (Pushkin) bored her. Food (especially pasta, for some reason) bored her. Music bored her. Her friends bored her. School really bored her. When her parents told her they would no longer search for her if she ran again—*some tough-love bullshit*, she calls it—she left them a note that said, *It's not your fault* and took off. Now she lives in Seattle, couch surfing and panhandling and meeting people she calls *fascinatingly weird*. She's been beaten up a couple of times (*all that orthodontic work shot to shit*), and she has a chronic cough that she treats with stolen cough syrup. But she's not bored. Not at all. She calls home (collect) on Mother's Day, Father's Day, her birthday and Christmas. *I'm not trying to hurt them*, she says. *I just don't want their life.* Seems like a pretty extreme way to deal with boredom, but then, I'm not a risk taker. I can't imagine running away from Mom and Verna. It makes me sick just to think about it. Sonia sounds really selfish. Maybe there's something she's not telling Mom, something horrific that would explain her behavior, but all I can do is transcribe what I hear.

I close Sonia's file and reread Meredith's email. Maybe *brusque* is the right word for it, as if she has no emotional stake in seeing me. My phone pings—Lucy's text says, **I got an email from her too. So yeah, let's go together. Not our café though. Downtown? I miss you too, sis.**

Our café. I smile and text back: **Monday @ Starbucks in PP Mkt? 2 pm.** As an afterthought, I add, **She doesn't sound very friendly.**

Maybe she's shy. But I'm curious. You?

Curious enough to meet her. I'll email her and get back to you.

I shoot Meredith an email and get a three-word response: See you then.

The rest of the week is predictable: hair salon and dog walking in the mornings, transcribing in the afternoons, dinner with Mom, watching movies or reading in the evenings, hanging out with the ladies on Sunday. This week's playlist: old musicals. We did a rousing chorus of "I'm Gonna Wash That Man Right Outta My Hair," which seemed deeply appropriate.

Shanti is there for a shampoo, and I ask her about Brad, the guy Annabeth thinks might be a pimp.

She shakes her head. "Not someone I know," she says, "but I'll ask around. In the meantime, tell her to be careful. Lots of weirdos out there. And lots of them look perfectly normal."

I nod as if I know what she's talking about.

Ben has accepted my emailed apology—his exact words were *No worries, mate*, and we're going to Skype soon, when we can figure out a good time. One night when Mom and I are sitting on the couch—Mom's reading and I'm watching old episodes of *Veronica Mars* on my computer—my phone pings. When I pick it up and read a text from Lucy that makes me laugh, Mom asks if I'm back in touch with Byron.

I shake my head. "Nope," I say.

She looks up from the gigantic tome she's reading and raises an eyebrow at me. "It's not like you to be so mysterious, Harry."

"Just a friend," I mumble, pulling my feet off her lap and standing up.

She nods and goes back to her book. In a way, I wish she would pry a bit, worm it out of me. Make me talk. At this point, I'm not even sure why I'm keeping it a secret. Maybe I'll tell her after I meet Meredith.

I don't know why I suggested the Pike Place Starbucks. It's crowded and noisy and full of tourists. I find Lucy at a table in a corner, and she asks how we're going to recognize Meredith. "No idea," I say. "Her emails weren't exactly chatty. I told her to look for a tiny Asian girl with long hair and a tall girl wearing a red Pearl Jam T-shirt."

Lucy and I sit and watch the crowd. Two o'clock comes and goes, and I'm beginning to think we've been stood up when a girl and a guy come in and start looking around instead of ordering coffee. The girl, who is shorter than me but not as short as Lucy, is very pale and thin. She's wearing a black-and-white-striped boat-neck top with black capris and black ballet flats. Très chic. A small black leather pack is slung over one shoulder. Everything about her is sharp: her nose, her chin, the bones of her wrists, her shoulder blades. Her hair is black and aggressively short, shorter than a pixie cut. Her eyebrows are heavy—Audrey Hepburn heavy, not unibrow heavy.

The guy she's with is about my height and slim, almost skinny, with a haircut like hers—as if they went to a salon and had their heads shaved at the same time, and now it's growing back. His hair is blond and curly, though, which makes it look as if he has a halo.

They spot us, and I wave as they walk over to our table. I stand up and say, "Meredith?"

She nods and smiles with her lips closed, as if she's afraid she has poppy seeds stuck between her teeth. "I'm so pleased to meet you," she says. "Hope you don't mind—I brought my friend, Alex."

"Hi, Alex," Lucy and I chorus. Alex shakes our hands. His palm is cool and dry, his grip firm. He's wearing a wrinkled pale-blue button-down shirt with the sleeves rolled up to his elbows, gray plaid shorts and checkered Vans. No socks.

Meredith turns to him and says, "I'd love an iced soy chai tea latte."

"Coming right up," Alex says. "You guys good?" he asks Lucy and me. When he smiles, I can see that his front teeth are crooked. Not snaggletooth crooked but noticeable.

Lucy and I nod and hold up our drinks. Meredith grabs a chair, pulls it over to our table and sits down. After she stares at us for a few moments, she says, "You'd never know, would you? That we were related."

"It's the Japanese thing," Lucy says. "But Harry looks a lot like my brother Adam. Same donor, different moms."

Meredith's gaze darts back and forth between Lucy and me. Her eyes are a very pale blue—like acid-washed denim. "So your moms are gay?"

"Mine are," Lucy says.

"Mine's not," I say. "She's a single mom by choice. What about yours?"

"Standard-issue suburban parents. I don't talk to them anymore."

"I'm sorry," I say.

"Don't be," Meredith replies. "I'm here now, meeting my sisters. That's what's important." She smiles. Her lips are thin, and it looks as if she never lost her baby teeth or, if she did, her adult teeth came in very small. I can understand if she doesn't smile a lot.

Alex comes back to the table with Meredith's drink and a lemonade for himself. He sits down between me and Meredith, who thanks him for the drink and gives him a kiss on the cheek.

"So, how many sibs have you found so far?" she asks. "Other than Adam."

"One more that I know of," Lucy says. "Ben, in Australia. He's awesome."

"And some Mormon guy—James something-or-other," I add.

"You didn't tell me about him." Lucy frowns at me.

"Mormons are so strange," Meredith says. "All those wives."

I stop myself before I launch into Mom's *not all Mormons are polygamists* speech. "He seems nice enough," I say instead, even though I never replied to his email and he hasn't tried to contact me again. For some reason, I feel like defending him. "Anyway, he lives in Florida somewhere. He just came back from Argentina."

"Probably trying to convert the heathen," Meredith says with a breathy laugh.

Alex says, "I lived next door to a Mormon family when I was little. Super nice people. Generous, kind. I spent a lot of time at their house."

A look passes between Alex and Meredith that I can't quite decipher. I think maybe he's telling her to back off about Mormons, but I could be wrong.

"Was that in Montana?" Lucy asks.

Alex shakes his head. "Texas. Montana came later, when I was six. That's where I met Meredith—in first grade."

"He puked Cream of Wheat all over the teacher's shoes on the first day of class. Miss Oakley, remember?"

Alex grimaces. "You never let me forget. I was so nervous. New city. New school. Meredith rescued me. Took me to the nurse's office. We've been friends ever since."

"Best friends," Meredith says, as if one of us has challenged her.

"So how'd you end up in Seattle?" I ask.

"We both needed to get out of Missoula, and I wanted to find my dad, so we headed west and ended up here."

"Wasn't your dad in Missoula?" Lucy says.

"I'm talking about my real dad. You know, our father. I'm eighteen now. I can look for him legally. Don't you want to meet him?"

I shake my head. So does Lucy.

"You sure?" Meredith says. "I mean, he's our father." Her eyebrows draw together.

"No he isn't," Lucy says. "He's our *donor*. There's a difference."

Meredith shrugs. "Suit yourself. But I'm sure he's around here somewhere. I've even got a picture. Wanna see it?" She starts to reach into her bag, and I put my hand on her arm to stop her. She flinches as if I have hurt her, which I'm sure I haven't.

"I'm sorry, Meredith," I say as she rubs her arm. "I'm just not ready."

"Me either," Lucy says. "I don't think my moms ever saw a picture. Did yours?" she asks me.

"I don't think so," I say. "If she did, she hasn't shown me. Seeing a picture changes things, don't you think? Makes it so much more personal, when really, it wasn't personal at all."

"I have to disagree," Meredith says. "It's deeply personal. When did you guys find out you were donor kids?"

"I don't remember," I say. "I've always known. So I must have been really little."

"Angela and Nori told me they started talking about my donor the minute I was born," Lucy adds. "Not that I understood until I was older, but it was never, like, announced. It was just part of who I was."

"I didn't find out until I was twelve," Meredith says. "I grew up believing a lie."

"Whoa," Lucy says. "That's rough."

"But you loved your dad—the man who raised you—didn't you?" I ask.

Meredith glares at me. "That's not the point. He betrayed me. My mom betrayed me. When they told me, all I could think about was finding my real dad. And now I can. I was hoping you'd want to share my journey. It would mean so much to me. To do this with my sisters."

Tears form in her pale eyes and hang on her thick black lashes. She grabs Lucy's hand in both of hers as a single tear makes its way down one pale cheek. "I feel like we've known each other forever." She turns to me. "And you too, Harry."

I don't know what to say. I don't feel that way at all. She's a stranger. A stranger with some of my DNA.

"I'm sorry," Lucy says. "It's just such a new idea. But maybe you're right. Can I think about it? Talk to my moms?"

"Of course," Meredith says, letting go of Lucy's hand. "It's an important decision. I've been thinking about it for a couple of years. I guess I should give you more than a couple of minutes to decide!" She laughs. "Alex says I'm

like a steamroller once I get going, don't you, sweetie?"
She reaches over and pats his cheek. Am I imagining it,
or does he look a bit uncomfortable?

"How long have you been in Seattle?" I ask. It's a lame
segue, I know, but I don't want to talk any more about
finding our donor.

"Almost a year," Alex says. "You?"

"Born and raised. Lucy too."

"Lucky you," he says. "Noticeably short on rednecks
out here. Compared to Texas and Montana. You don't see
a lot of pickup trucks with gun racks outside the Whole
Foods market."

"More like Smart cars with *Things Go Better With Kale*
bumper stickers," I say.

Lucy giggles and Alex smiles—a wide, genuine, eye-
crinkling smile—and I notice that his eyes are a very deep,
dark blue, the color of the lapis lazuli stone in my favorite
ring.

"Funny," he says to me, and I'm sure I blush.

"We should go, Alex." Meredith gets up from the
table. "I need to get to work."

"Where do you work?" Lucy asks.

"I've got two jobs," Meredith says. "One at a dance
store and one at a health-food store."

"A dance store?" Lucy says. "Which one?"

"Pirouette."

"I love that store! Nori says we've spent enough money
there to buy a new car."

"You dance?"

"Every day since I was, like, three."

Meredith links arms with Lucy and they leave the coffee shop, heads together, laughing.

"After you," Alex says with a small bow, and we head up the hill.

"She's a good person," he says as we walk. "A good friend." Is he a mind reader? How else could he know that I haven't exactly warmed to Meredith?

"Do you think she'll find him?" I ask. "Our donor?"

"I don't know. She's sure he's here. He went to med school here, but he could be anywhere. She's reached out through the DSR but hasn't had any response, I guess. Now all we can do is wait."

We. I wonder if they're more than best friends. He seems like a nice guy. Smart, funny, considerate. She seems—odd, for want of a better word.

When we get to the top of the hill, Lucy is waiting for us, but Meredith is nowhere in sight. I can tell by the way Alex's head swivels that he is looking for her.

"Looks like she ditched us," I say.

"She said she had a bus to catch," Lucy tells us. "She didn't want to be late for work."

"And neither do I," Alex says. "The dogs hate to wait."

"What dogs?" Lucy asks. "You have dogs?"

"No, not right now. I volunteer at an animal shelter. When I'm not bussing tables. Guess which job I prefer." He laughs.

"That's so cool," Lucy says.

"Bussing tables?"

Lucy punches him lightly on the arm. "No, silly. Working at a shelter."

"It is," Alex says. "Wish I got paid for it." He pauses. "You know, Meredith was really nervous about meeting you guys today. Finding you means a lot to her. I'm sure she'll be in touch. Or I will, if you give me your numbers."

We nod like bobblehead dolls, give him our numbers and then watch him walk away.

Beside me, Lucy exhales loudly. "That was...intense."

"Very."

"What do you think?"

"About what?"

"Meredith. Alex."

I shake my head. "I have no idea."

We trudge up Pike Street in silence. When we get close to my bus stop, Lucy asks, "Are you going to tell your mom now?"

I stop walking and look over at her—my little sister— and realize that I'm glad she's here with me, glad that we met Meredith together, glad that she's in my life. "Yes," I say. "Yes, I am."

FIVE

WHEN I GET HOME, Verna is sitting on the couch, crocheting. Mom is in her office, but she comes out when she hears me.

"There you are," she says. "Verna's staying for dinner and some Scrabble. There's chicken in the oven. Could you make a salad?"

"Sure," I say. Verna eats dinner with us quite often, but there's something about the atmosphere in the room—some tension between them, maybe—that makes me wonder if they're staging some kind of intervention. If so, they're in for a big surprise.

I wash my hands, then chop up tomatoes and peppers and cucumbers for a Greek salad, all the while trying to formulate a graceful way of introducing the fact that I have searched for, and found, some half-siblings.

When we sit down for dinner, we talk about the usual stuff—the Sunday ladies (Bonnie is in detox again), Mom's work (one of her girls has been arrested, another has returned home), how many more squares Verna has to crochet before she has enough for an afghan (seventeen). After dinner, I clear off the dishes to make room for Scrabble at the table, and when we're all sitting again, Mom fires the opening salvo. "Verna and I are worried about you, Harry."

Verna nods and holds the bag of tiles out to me. "You've been very distant lately," she says. "You still mooning over Byron?"

I shake my head. Now is not the time to tell Verna that *mooning* has more than one meaning.

"Then what is it?" Mom asks. "You know I don't like to pry, but it's just not like you."

"What isn't like me?"

"Being secretive. Disappearing without telling anyone where you're going. Texting all the time. Shutting us out. Does it have anything to do with the card that's gone from the fridge?"

I arrange my tiles on the little wooden rack. I love the feel of the tiles, the clicking sound they make in the bag. *Q-A-W-J-I-O-O*. Good thing Mom is going first. She puts the word *BREATHE* on the board, and Verna writes down her points. Even I know a sign when I see one.

I take a deep breath and let the words rush out as I exhale. "I went on DSR to look for my half-siblings, and I've found two sisters and three brothers so far, and my two sisters are here."

There's a moment of silence. For once, they are speechless. It doesn't last. Mom says, "Holy shit," and Verna lets out a hoot.

And then come the questions:

"When can we meet them?"

"How old are they?"

"What are their names?"

"Where are your three brothers?"

"Do you have any pictures on your phone?"

"Why didn't you tell us sooner?"

The last question comes from Verna, and before I can answer it, Mom says, "I can understand why you didn't, Harry. This is the kind of thing you need to process before you share it." She shoots Verna a look that I know all too well: *Don't push it*, the look says.

Verna says, "Well, we're glad to know now, aren't we, Della?"

"Absolutely," Mom says. "Harry, it's your turn. Take your time." And I know she's not just talking about Scrabble. I put down *JAW* and then Verna plays *BANDAGE* and complains that she could have had a Bingo if she'd had an *I* to make *BADINAGE*. Mom tells her to stop whining and write her score down. Business as usual.

"I met Lucy first," I finally say, "but I heard from a Mormon guy named James before that. He's older, and he lives in Florida. It's weird to think that I'm related to a Mormon." I expect Mom to lecture me about the importance of keeping an open mind, but she just nods and I continue. "Lucy's fifteen, and she's half Japanese. She's a ballet dancer. Her brother Adam is at college in Portland. And she found another brother, Ben, in Australia. Or he found her—I'm not sure which. Her moms are Nori and Angela. I only met Meredith today. She's from Montana. She's eighteen. Really, I barely know any of them."

Mom plays *MOANED*. "That's a lot to take in. When did you say you met Lucy?"

"Just over a week ago. She's pretty cool. Really friendly and bubbly. Meredith—not so much."

"What do you mean?"

"She wanted to show me a picture of our donor, and I stopped her by grabbing her arm. Not hard or anything, but she didn't like it."

"Because you grabbed her arm?" Verna asks.

"I guess so. Or maybe because I didn't want to see a picture of him. I didn't even know you could get pictures of donors."

"It's optional," Mom says, "but I can understand why you wouldn't want to see a picture. I never did."

"Meredith's convinced that he's here—in Seattle— because he went to medical school here."

"Could be," Mom says. "But he could be anywhere. Do you want to find him too?" She doesn't sound upset, just curious.

I shake my head. "Neither does Lucy. Not yet, anyway. Siblings are all I can handle right now." I look down at my Scrabble tray and realize I haven't picked up new letters. I pull an *R* and a *P* from the bag and put them on my tray. Then I stare at the board and can't think of a single word to make. I must stare for a while because Verna says, "It's your turn, Harry."

"Sorry. I can't concentrate. Maybe you two should play without me."

Mom gets up and puts the kettle on. Verna picks up her crocheting and says, "I'd like to hear more about these girls, Harry."

I shoot Mom a desperate look. I can't talk anymore tonight. I'm exhausted, and I want to check my phone to see if I've got any texts from my sisters. *My sisters.* Sounds so strange.

"Let's have tea and play some crib, Verna," Mom says. "I think Harry's tired."

Verna nods. "Give this old lady a kiss then," she says, leaning toward me. "And don't be late for work tomorrow." I kiss her on the cheek and give Mom a quick hug before I head to my room.

"Thanks," I whisper.

"Sleep well, Harry," she says.

When I get to my room, I check my phone for messages (nothing) and get under the covers in my clothes. My last thought before I fall sleep is, I hope Alex calls.

But it's not Alex who calls me; it's Meredith. My phone rings just as I'm leaving the salon on Tuesday. When I answer, the first thing she says is, "I can't talk for long. I'm on my break."

"Okay," I say. I hate it when people make or answer calls and then say they're too busy to talk. It's so rude.

"Look, I'm sorry about leaving without saying goodbye to you on Monday." Her voice wavers, and it sounds as if she's going to cry.

"Don't worry about it," I say. "It was a weird situation."

"I'd like to see you and Lucy again. Maybe Thursday morning? Before I go to work? I have to be there at noon."

She sounds so eager that I can't bring myself to say no. And who knows? Maybe Monday was just a bad day for her. Maybe she had PMS, or she got shit on by one of the million gulls in Seattle. Giving her another chance seems like the right thing to do. And besides, maybe she'll bring Alex.

"I work at a hair salon in the mornings, but you could come by and I'll take a break. Not sure if Lucy can make it—she might be at class—but I'll text her."

I give her the address before I can think better of it and suggest eleven as a good time. If it goes well, we can meet again soon. If not—well, we'll see.

When I get home, Mom is out, and I make a ham sandwich before beginning another transcription. I text Lucy about meeting Meredith on Thursday.

My phone pings. Lucy. **Where and when?** I text her back with the address and time. What's that expression Verna uses? *In for a penny, in for a pound.* Which basically means "go big or go home." Well, at least I have a home to go to.

"Lucy and Meredith are coming by this morning," I tell Verna on Thursday when I get to the salon. Keeping it casual, as if having my sisters drop by was a routine occurrence. "Hope that's okay."

Verna stops folding towels and gazes at me, her head slightly tilted. "Of course it's okay. But why here? Why not at home? I'm sure your mother would like to meet them."

I punch the salon's voice-mail code into the phone and start listening to the messages. Appointments, cancellations, questions about products and prices. The usual.

"Meredith works," I say, which is true. "This is the only time she could come. I told her I was working too. But I figured you wouldn't mind if I took a break." I glance at the appointment book. "It's not super busy."

Part of me wants Verna to say, *No, you can't take a break*, but that's ridiculous. It's not like I punch a time clock or anything. She nods and goes back to folding towels. I spend the next hour returning calls, doing a couple of shampoos and sweeping the floor so often that Verna takes the broom away from me. I want to scrub the sinks and dust every flat surface, but I control myself. It's not that I'm ashamed of the salon or of Verna. I'm not trying to impress Meredith and Lucy. That's not the way I was raised. And I don't know them well enough to know what would impress them anyway. So why do I feel so antsy?

"What's that stupid expression?" Verna says after she notices me straightening the pens and the appointment book for the tenth time. "*It is what it is.* Stop fussing and take out the trash. It's pickup day tomorrow." She smiles at me and starts drying Mrs. Wallace's hair.

I take the trash out into the alley behind the salon, and when I come back in, Meredith and Lucy are there, standing by the battered Ikea desk that passes for a reception table. The desk was mine when I was about eleven. You can still see where I wrote my name in glitter nail polish.

I brush off some stray hairs that are clinging to my T-shirt and say, "Hey, guys, sorry about that. Just, you know, working."

"This salon is adorable," Meredith says. "So retro." Today she is wearing a plain white shirt tucked into dark skinny jeans. Her red patent-leather belt matches her shoes. Lucy has on a very full, very short turquoise skirt and a bright orange crop top that shows off her toned midriff. On her feet are Dr. Seuss Converse high-tops—Thing One and Thing Two. Once again, I am the drab sister.

Verna finishes up with Mrs. Wallace, who is telling a long story about her son, who has just gotten out of jail, where he got his GED.

"You remember Lenny, don't you, honey?" she says to me when Verna swings the chair around.

"Sure do, Mrs. Wallace," I reply. "Glad he's out." Lenny was a few years ahead of me in school. Good-looking but a total stoner. Got busted for dealing. Big surprise.

Her eyes widen when she sees Meredith and Lucy. "And who are these lovely ladies?"

"We're Harry's—"

Before Lucy can say "sisters," Verna says, "These are Harry's friends. Why don't you girls grab a soda or make yourselves some coffee while I settle up with Mrs. W.?"

Verna helps Mrs. Wallace out of the chair (she's not a small woman) and over to the desk to pay her bill while I lead Lucy and Meredith to the tiny room in the back of the salon that holds a small fridge, a coffeemaker and a stacked washer-dryer combo.

"There's coffee or"—I open the fridge and peer inside—"Diet Pepsi?"

"Diet Pepsi, please," Lucy says.

"Do you have bottled water?" Meredith asks. "Diet drinks are full of chemicals, you know. And I don't drink coffee."

Why am I not surprised?

"Just tap water. Sorry. You want some?"

Meredith shakes her head as Lucy pops open her can of soda and takes a long swig. "Ahhh." Lucy wipes her mouth with the back of her hand. "So good."

We go back into the salon, where Verna is closing the door after Mrs. Wallace. "Got everything you need?" she says.

I nod. Lucy burps, giggles and then apologizes. Meredith looks around and says, "Are those vintage?" She points at the three swivel chairs, which are upholstered in faded red vinyl.

"If by *vintage* you mean they came with the shop when I bought it fifty years ago, then yes." Verna laughs. "Haven't changed a thing."

"Cool," Meredith says, sitting in one of the chairs and twirling languidly from side to side. "I love the lino."

I look down at the floor, which I've always thought was hideous. Speckled white background (now gray) with weird atomic-looking red and black starbursts. I sit on the loveseat and try to see what Meredith sees, but I can't. I love the salon, but it still seems shabby to me.

"Believe it or not, I get people coming in all the time, trying to buy my chairs." Verna chuckles. "Not to use in salons, but to put in their living rooms. And one fellow wanted a tile from the floor to frame. Can you imagine?"

Meredith nods solemnly. "Totally."

Lucy, who has been turning pirouettes on the ugly lino, sits beside me on the loveseat and watches Meredith twirl. Verna sits in one of the other chairs and turns to Lucy. "Harry tells me you're a dancer."

Lucy nods. "Since I was three."

"Me too," Meredith says. "But not ballet. I started with ballet, but I found it much too"—she searches for the word—"too rigid. So many rules. And toe shoes? Sheer torture." She turns to me. "Did you ever take ballet, Harry?" Her close-mouthed smile is almost a simper. She must realize that I'm not exactly ballet material. Too tall, for one thing. Probably too heavy too, by ballet standards.

I shake my head. "Basketball's more my thing," I say, even though I haven't played in years. Verna shoots me a look that I know means *What is going on here?*

"It's such an incredible commitment," Meredith continues. "A calling, almost. For a while I thought that's what I'd do with my life, but after a couple of years in a company—well, let's just say it's not for me. I got sick of starving myself and competing with other dancers. So toxic."

"You were in a company?" Lucy sounds awestruck. "Where?"

"Denver." She names a company I've never heard of, but clearly Lucy is impressed.

"Don't you miss it?" Lucy asks.

Meredith shrugs. "Sometimes. But I'm focusing on different things now."

"Like what?" Verna asks.

"Finding our dad. Working. Saving money."

"Your dad."

"Didn't Harry tell you? That's why I'm in Seattle."

Verna nods. "She did mention it. Seems like a fool's errand if he doesn't want to be found."

I expect Meredith to either burst into tears or get mad or both, but all she says is, "Well, then, I guess I'm a fool." She smiles at Verna without showing her teeth.

"How are you going about this search?" Verna asks. "I assume he's not registered on DSR, or you'd already have found each other. And how can you be sure he's here?"

"No, he's not on DSR," Meredith says, "but I have a gut feeling that he never left Seattle. I don't know why. And I have to start somewhere." She pulls out her phone, taps it a couple of times and holds it out to Lucy. "I set up a Facebook page to find him. And a Twitter account. I'm going to post a video on YouTube too. Anything I can think of to connect with him."

Lucy peers at the screen. "You gotta see this, Harry," she says. "You're not going to believe it." She hands me the phone, and my curiosity gets the better of me. Half of the cover image under the familiar blue line is a picture of a little girl sitting in a swing. Her dark hair is in pigtails, and she is staring solemnly at the camera. Meredith, I assume. The other half of the picture is a faded headshot of a young man with dark wavy hair, heavy eyebrows and dark eyes. He is smiling very slightly. As far as I can tell, his teeth are a normal size. The name of the page is *Have You Seen My Dad?* The profile picture is a recent photo of an unsmiling Meredith.

I stare at the man in the photo. My donor. Not my dad, I remind myself. He looks nice. Intelligent. Not super good-looking but not ugly either. Sort of average-looking. He looks like me. Or should I say, I look like him. I am the only daughter here who does. I feel a momentary jolt of recognition and a strange sense of... excitement. Something I hadn't expected to feel.

Below the cover photo are posts, lots of posts.

Posts from people who say they've sighted him in Paris or Singapore or Toronto.

Posts from other donor children, some encouraging, some telling Meredith to leave it alone.

My face pops out at me from a post, and I gasp. The picture was taken from a distance, but it's clearly Lucy and me at Starbucks, the first time we met Meredith. She must have taken it before she came over to the table. That's so creepy. Or maybe Alex took it, which is even creepier. Underneath the photo it says, *Meeting my sisters for the first time. Hope they like me!*

"You put us on your page?" I glare at Meredith, who has stopped twirling. "Without asking our permission?"

Meredith shrugs. "I wanted him to know that it's not just about me."

"But it *is* just about you," I say. "Lucy and I don't want to meet him." I remember that split second of excitement and wonder if I am lying. Maybe I do want to meet him, but I'm not about to admit it.

"I know *you* don't want to meet him. But you really shouldn't speak for other people." Meredith bares her tiny teeth in what I suppose is a smile. "Right, Lucy?"

Lucy stares at the floor and mumbles something that sounds like "I don't know anymore."

I nudge Lucy with my elbow, and she looks up at me. "Don't be mad," she says. "Meredith and I have been talking about it a lot. Maybe it is a good idea to meet him. I'm not sure." Her gaze darts between Meredith and me, and I can see how much she wants this to be okay, for the three of us to be like the sisters from *Little Women* or *Pride and Prejudice* or something. Loving, kind, devoted to each other. Not bitchy and manipulative and competitive. Right now, I feel more like one of the nasty sisters from *King Lear*. Which probably makes Lucy poor Cordelia.

"I'm not mad," I say, although I am. "Just confused. I thought we agreed it wasn't a good idea right now."

"Meredith says we need closure."

"Closure? Why?"

"Because of, like, the pain of growing up without a father." Lucy's eyes dart away from mine again.

I want to yell at her, shake her, remind her that she has two perfectly good parents, but right then the bell over the door jingles, and Miss Mathers, our oldest and sweetest client, totters in, pushing her walker and wafting a cloud of what she calls her "signature scent," Yardley's English Lavender.

With Miss Mathers is her caregiver, Consuela, a tiny, cheerful Ecuadorian woman whose long dark braid is streaked with gray. They are here for their weekly shampoo and blow-dry. Verna is the only one who understands how to keep Miss Mathers's waist-length hair aloft in an elaborate updo for seven days. Every week, Verna suggests a cut. Every week, Miss Mathers says, *A woman's hair is her crowning glory.* I happen to think she's right.

I jump up and help Miss Mathers take off her coat, a heavy tweed that she wears year-round. She smiles at me with her dazzling false teeth. As I settle her in the shampoo chair next to Consuela and start to take out all her hairpins, Meredith and Lucy edge toward the door.

"You don't have to go," I say, but I wish they would—well, I wish Meredith would—and I wonder if it shows on my face.

"I have to get to work," Meredith says. "And you're obviously busy."

"I've got a class," Lucy adds.

"Nice to meet you, girls," Verna calls out.

"You too," they chorus as they leave.

"Toodle-oo!!" says Miss Mathers.

SIX

A FEW DAYS later, I get a text from Alex. **Wanna come dog walking this aft?**

I haven't heard from Lucy or Meredith since they came to the salon, and I haven't contacted either of them. I think we all need time to think about what should happen next. Well, I do, anyway. I've spent a lot of time staring at the picture of my donor, as if he can help me figure out what to do. So far, he hasn't. Dog walking with a cute guy is just what I need.

Sure, I text back. **Where and when?**

Meet me at the shelter at 3. The shelter's address is followed by an emoticon of a smiling dog.

See you then, I write. It's already one o'clock. I need to have a shower, shave my legs, wash and dry my hair, choose an appropriate dog-and-guy-friendly outfit and take the bus to the shelter. All my clothes seem deeply inadequate, if not downright crappy. The best I can do is faded green shorts, a cute plaid shirt and a pair of red Asics runners. I put my hair up into a high ponytail and make sure that neither my lip gloss nor my mascara is smeared. It's just a dog walk, I keep telling myself. Not a date. But it's been a long time since I've felt this strange combination of excitement and uncertainty. The last time was when I had to read my prize-winning essay about climate change to my whole school. If I'm being honest, I never felt it much with Byron. There was never any uncertainty. Or an awful lot of excitement. What I'm feeling now is not an entirely pleasant sensation—I feel a bit light-headed—and it's absolutely not rational. You're going dog walking, I tell myself, not out for dinner and a movie, for god's sake.

When I get to the shelter, I'm sweaty and nauseated. I'd like to think it's from the bus ride, but the minute I see Alex, standing in front of the shelter with a very large, very shaggy black dog, I know I'm kidding myself.

"Hi, Harry. This is Churchill," Alex says when I walk up to them. "Sit, Churchill."

Churchill sits, drooling, and regards me patiently.

"Hey, Churchill," I say. "How's it going?"

"Better now that you're here," Alex says in a deep, rumbly voice. Churchill's voice. "I need you to rub my belly."

"Really?" I laugh. "But I hardly know you." Are we flirting already? It seems too good to be true.

"Lie down, Churchill," Alex says in his regular voice. Churchill complies, then rolls over onto his back and bares his belly. His tongue lolls out of his mouth, and he appears to be grinning. I squat down and give his belly a good rub, wishing for the thousandth time that Mom would let me have a dog.

I straighten, and Churchill leaps to his feet and starts pulling Alex down the street.

"Not so fast, big guy," Alex says. "He's got a lot of energy. Doesn't know how to heel. I'm working on that, but it's slow. He used to live on a big fenced property. Never got leash trained."

"Why is he at the shelter?" I ask.

"His owner died, I think. The heirs sold the property and brought Churchill here. He's a great dog, but he goes off like a rocket if he sees a cat or a squirrel. Nearly yanked my arm out of its socket once. But he's kind of getting the hang of the leash. And he's getting better with basic commands."

I walk beside Alex, with Churchill yawing back and forth in front of us. Occasionally the leash gets tangled in our legs, and once I have to grab Alex to keep from falling over. Does he hold on to me a bit longer than necessary? I think so, but I can't be sure. I start to hope that Churchill will trip me again. When we arrive at the park, which is an off-leash area, Alex unclips Churchill from the leash. He takes off toward some other dogs, and Alex says, "Meredith told me you don't want to meet your dad."

Wow, this guy really cuts to the chase. Maybe I'm reading this all wrong. Maybe he's Meredith's emissary, and he's not interested in me at all.

"He's not my dad. He's my donor." I'm still not ready to tell anybody I might have changed my mind.

"Yeah, I get that."

"So why doesn't she?"

He shrugs. "Maybe she just needs someone to share the experience with. Someone who understands."

"But I don't understand. Really, I don't. I didn't grow up longing for a dad."

"Well, she did."

So now I'm supposed to feel guilty that I have a great mom?

"What was her mom like?" I ask.

"Hard to say. I mean, I'd go to Meredith's house and her mom would be all *Have some milk and cookies*, but in private? You never really know, do you? Maybe it was a totally different story. But her folks were really good to me, especially her dad."

I think of the girls in Mom's study—all the reasons they run away and end up homeless. Maybe I should try to be a bit more compassionate toward Meredith. A bit kinder.

We stand in silence and watch Churchill race around the park.

Finally Alex says, "I'm sorry I brought it up. I didn't ask you here to get you to change your mind."

"No? Then why did you ask me?" There's something about Alex that invites openness. Unlike Meredith, he seems incapable of deviousness. I turn to look at him and see that he is blushing, which is incredibly sweet.

"Because I like you," he says.

"You've only met me once," I say, although why I want to argue with him is beyond me.

"And I liked you. Is that so hard to believe?" The blush is receding, and he is grinning at me. "Don't tell me you're one of those girls with tragically low self-esteem."

I laugh. "Not tragically low. Just average." Like the rest of me, I think.

"Well, you passed the belly-rub test. I can't be with a girl who won't rub a dog's belly."

"Well, yeah," I say. "Belly rubbing is the key to a good relationship." I put my fingers in my mouth and let loose a piercing whistle. All the dogs in the park stop running and look at me. "Churchill, come!" I yell, and he races toward us. Alex hands me a dog treat, and I get Churchill to sit and shake a paw before I give it to him. Then he puts his paws on my shoulders and licks my face before he runs off again.

"Looks like Churchill's got a new best friend," Alex says. "I feel so betrayed. And jealous. I always wanted to be able to whistle like that."

"My mom taught me. Her whistle is epic. Almost painful. Better than any rape whistle, she claims. I could teach you. You just have to know where to put your lips and fingers and tongue."

The minute it is out of my mouth, I realize that it sounds pretty, well, dirty. Alex snorts and says, "As the actress said to the bishop." We both start to laugh, and we can't stop. Tears stream down our faces, and Churchill barrels over to investigate. He obligingly jumps up and licks the tears and snot from my face. Talk about a memorable first date. If that's what this is.

Alex and I circle the park, keeping an eye on Churchill, who is romping around with a fluffy white dog the size of his head. Every now and again he bounds over to us, like a canine chaperone, begs for a treat and bounds off again. My hand brushes Alex's as we walk, and I have to remind myself that this is only the second time we have met. It's too soon for hand-holding, isn't it? Byron and I knew each other for years before we held hands. But this is different. Really different.

"What happens if Churchill doesn't get adopted?" I ask, even though I think I know the answer: he'll be put down. The thought brings tears to my eyes as I watch Churchill tear around the park with his tiny friend in pursuit.

"He's a great dog," Alex says firmly. "Someone will take him. And he's only been at the shelter a week."

"How do you deal with it?"

"Deal with what?"

"You know—if a dog has to be put down."

"It's only happened to me once so far. And it was brutal. That's not going to happen to Churchill. Not if I can help it."

He calls Churchill over before I can ask what he means, attaches his leash and says we need to get back to the shelter. We walk in silence for a while, and I wonder if somehow I've completely blown it. But then he says, "I'll be walking Churchill again soon. Probably Thursday. You in?"

"Absolutely," I say. "I'll even teach you to whistle."

"Meredith might come too, if she's not working."

"Cool." No way am I going to tell him that I'm not a big fan of his best friend, even if she is my half-sister. Maybe it will be good for me to spend more time with her. Maybe I've misjudged her. If he likes her, there might be something I'm missing.

When we get back to the shelter, he says, "I have to stay and do some more work here—cleaning out the kennels, filling water bowls, that kind of thing. The dog walking is the fun part. So—same time on Thursday?" He smiles and I smile back. We stand there like two grinning idiots as Churchill winds his leash around our ankles. I extricate myself without falling over, give Churchill a final belly rub and head toward the bus stop.

Suddenly Thursday seems a very long way off.

On the bus back home I get a text from Lucy: **Can u come over?**

Over where? I reply.

My house. I need to talk to u.

I pause a minute before I reply, and another message comes in from her: **My moms aren't home.**

K. What's your address? What bus should I take?

She gives me directions, and I tell her I'll be there as soon as I can. She doesn't tell me what's wrong, but if I had to guess, I'd say it has something to do with Meredith.

Lucy's house is the kind my mom has always wanted but can't afford—a moss-green Craftsman bungalow, with a large porch, stone-covered pillars and shingle siding. The wide front stairs lead up to a deep-burgundy door with a silver knocker in the shape of a giant bee. The door opens before I have a chance to knock, and Lucy grabs my hand and pulls me inside. Her outfit of the day includes a straw fedora, which is cute but odd. Who wears a hat in their own house?

The front hallway is cool and dim. As I follow Lucy through to the kitchen at the back of the house, I notice many of the features my mom has been obsessing about for years: wooden wall panels, exposed rafters, stained-glass windows, hardwood floors, a brick fireplace. The kitchen has obviously been renovated—there's a bright-red gas stove, a huge island with a sink in it, windows everywhere.

"Let's go out on the deck," Lucy says. She leads me through french doors onto a multi-level wooden deck that overlooks a lush back garden. A large brick-red umbrella shades a round wooden table that has a tray on it with glasses and a pitcher of what looks like pink lemonade. "Want some?" Lucy asks.

I nod and say, "That's some garden."

"Nori's pride and joy," Lucy says as she hands me a glass of lemonade. "It's been in *Seattle Magazine.* Even won some award—best of Seattle's small gardens or something. You'd think she'd be sick of gardening after working in other people's gardens all the time, but she says this is her sanctuary. She even made a special place for Angela to meditate in. Do you want to see it? It's really cool. Very Japanese."

She starts to get up, and I put a hand on her arm. "What did you want to talk about?"

She sits down and stares into her glass of lemonade. "I did something stupid," she says. "Really stupid."

I don't say anything—Mom always says that silence is actually the best way to get someone to talk. As we sit, I notice that Lucy is crying. I can't actually see her face— the brim of the fedora hides it—but I can see drops falling on the wooden table.

"What's wrong, Lucy?" I ask. "It can't be that bad."

She looks up at me, her face streaked with tears, and takes off her hat. Her beautiful curtain of silky black hair is gone. What's left is a spiky pixie cut, just like Meredith's. I say, "Holy shit!" and she starts to wail.

"Angela and Nori are so mad at me. They're saying that Meredith is a bad influence. They don't want me hanging out with her—or you—until they've met both of you.

I said you had nothing to do with it, but they're getting all overprotective, and I'm afraid you guys won't want to meet them and—"

Before she can get herself any more worked up, I pull my chair over to hers and put my arms around her. It's like hugging a child, she's so small, and she looks more like a little kid than ever—a sad, confused little kid. We are sitting like this when the french doors open and a small wiry woman in jeans and a dirty white T-shirt steps onto the deck. Behind her is a tall tanned woman in a sky-blue sleeveless dress. Her long hair hangs in a braid down her back. Neither woman is smiling—they actually look pretty pissed—but the tall one's eyes widen when she sees me, and she gasps. I've forgotten how much I look like her son, Adam. It must be a shock to see someone who could be his twin.

I stand up and say, "Hi, I'm Harriet. I love your house. Craftsman, right? My mom loves them. Yours is gorgeous. And the garden is amazing."

As I babble, I reach out and shake their hands. First Angela's dry, cool one, then Nori's dirty one. Lucy says, "We're having lemonade. You guys want some?"

Nori and Angela look at each other, and I can practically see the thoughts arc between them. *Best of a bad situation. Get to know this girl. Try not to be hostile. We don't want to come off like assholes.*

"Sure, honey," Angela says. "That would be lovely." I bet she's the softie and Nori is the enforcer. Nori shrugs, and the two moms sit down while Lucy runs into the kitchen for more glasses. I notice she's put her fedora back on.

"So, Harriet, do you live nearby?" Nori asks.

"Not really. I was on the bus, going home from the animal shelter, and Lucy texted. I just invited myself over. Hope that's okay."

Angela nods. "We like Lucy to have friends over. But I'm sure you can understand that we're a bit"—she pauses—"a bit perplexed by recent events."

Nori snorts. "Perplexed doesn't even begin to cover it! Have you seen her hair? She's never had a haircut in her life. And now it's all gone. And all because your sister"—she almost spits out the word—"made her cut it."

"She didn't *make* me cut it." Lucy has returned with the glasses, which she fills for Angela and Nori. "She was watching me put my hair in a bun for dance class and she asked me why I didn't just cut it off. She used to dance, and her hair was long. She said it would be freeing."

"And is it?" Nori asks.

Lucy sits down and sips her lemonade. Then she takes off her hat and runs her fingers over her head. "I don't know. Maybe. It's weird to feel a breeze on my neck. And it's lighter, for sure."

She sounds so hesitant that I pipe up, "I think it's kinda cute. And it'll grow, right?"

Nori glares at me. "I cut my hair off when Lucy was a baby. I've always regretted it." She undoes her ponytail and shakes her head. Her thick hair falls to her shoulders. Jet black streaked with gray.

"It's just hair, Nori," Lucy says, but she doesn't sound convinced. She looks like a baby bird—fuzzy and vulnerable. "Can we drop it?"

Angela sighs. "We're still concerned about, well, about the influence your sisters are having on you." She looks over at me apologetically. "We need to get to know you, Harriet. You and Meredith. You can understand that, can't you?"

"Yeah, I guess so," I say. "My mom's the same way."

"Overprotective?" Lucy glares at her parents.

I laugh. "Yeah. You could say that. She knows too much about bad parents."

"Why is that?" Nori asks.

No way I'm telling her that my mom ran away from her own parents when she was younger than me, so all I say is, "Her work. She's a sociologist. She studies the lives of homeless girls, runaways. When she's not lusting after Craftsman houses."

Nori and Angela laugh. Even Lucy cracks a smile.

Nori stands up and says, "I'm going to have a shower. It was nice to meet you, Harriet. Sorry for the rough start."

"No problem," I say. "And call me Harry. Everyone else does."

She nods and heads inside.

"So now that you've met us," Angela says, "do you think maybe you and your mom could come for dinner soon?

We'll invite Meredith and her friend Alex. Eat some great food, get to know each other."

"Sure," I say. "That would be awesome." Any opportunity to see Alex seems good to me.

"Can Verna come too?" Lucy asks. "She's kind of like Harry's grandma. And she's met Meredith and me already."

"Plus she could bring her famous *tres leches* cake," I add. "It's amazing."

"Verna's awesome," Lucy adds. "She runs this totally retro hair salon."

"More the merrier, I suppose," Angela says. "Especially if there's cake. But for the record, Lucy, we're still not happy about your impulsive behavior. Or Meredith's part in it. We'll discuss it later."

Lucy grimaces, and I get up to leave. "Thanks for the lemonade," I say. "I'd better get home before Mom starts to worry. And it's my turn to make dinner."

Angela nods approvingly. I don't think she and Nori are going to be worrying about me leading Lucy astray. Anyone with half a brain can see I'm no threat. Time will tell about Meredith though.

After a flurry of texts, our family dinner is set up for Wednesday, the night before I'm due to meet Alex again. Verna is on board with making a cake, and Mom buys wine.

I am about to buy flowers for Angela and Nori when I remember Nori's garden. *Coals to Newcastle*, Verna would say. Like giving a bottle of wine to a vintner. Or bread to a baker. But I think I should take something. Then I have a moment of inspiration. Last year, Verna and I picked strawberries and made jam. It's delicious, and we've been kind of rationing it out. I was too depressed to go picking this year, and Verna didn't want to go alone, so we didn't replenish our stock, but maybe we have some left. I rummage around in the cupboard and find one solitary unopened jar. I don't think Mom will mind if I take it. It's for a good cause, after all. There's a label on it—not a fancy one, just an office label—that says *Strawbs 2014* in Verna's scribbly handwriting. I find a red pen and decorate the label with drawings of tiny berries. Then I tie a scrap of red ribbon around the top of the jar, and voilà! The perfect hostess gift.

SEVEN

WHEN WE GET to Lucy's house on Wednesday night, I am nervous. What if all the moms hate each other? What if I get into a fight with Meredith? What if Mom doesn't like Alex? I keep telling myself that it'll be fine—we'll all be on our best behavior, after all—but I have to fight a desire to turn around and run away. Verna must sense my uneasiness; she rubs my back as we mount the stairs.

"One may as well be hung for a sheep as a lamb," she says as I reach up to bang the bee knocker against the door. She has an endless store of weird expressions—one for every occasion, it seems, although I can't figure out how this one applies.

Lucy opens the door, looking like a child bride in some New Age cult. Her ankle-length dress is white and lacy. Her sandals are silver Birkenstocks. She is wearing a garland of small white flowers in her hair (or what's left of her hair). I introduce her to Mom, and she hugs us all, one after the other.

"Everyone's out back," Lucy says. "Meredith and Alex are getting the garden tour. And Angela wants to give you the house tour, Ms...."

When she hesitates, Mom says, "Call me Della. And I'd love a tour."

"Della," Lucy repeats. "That's so pretty."

She leads us to the kitchen, where Angela is washing some salad greens at the sink. Verna puts the cake down on the counter, and Angela dries her hands for the next round of introductions, this time with more handshaking and less hugging.

"Hope white is okay," Mom says, holding up the bottle of wine.

"And I brought you some jam," I say. "Verna and I made it last summer."

I hand Angela the jam and she says, "This is lovely, Harry. So thoughtful." She beams at me. "Strawberry is my favorite. Lucy's too. And we're having salmon, Della, so the wine is perfect. You're not vegetarians, are you? Or vegan?"

"God forbid," Mom says, and Angela laughs.

"These days you have to be so careful. No gluten, no dairy, nothing with a face."

"We eat everything," Mom says. "Right, Harry?"

"Pretty much. Except okra. We hate okra."

"Not on the menu," Angela says. "Harry tells me you're a Craftsman fan, Della. Let me show you and Verna the house."

The three of them wander off to admire the wainscoting or something, and Lucy and I head toward the back deck, where the table is covered with a blue-and-white-striped tablecloth held in place by weights in the shape of silver bees. The water glasses are embossed with bees. The napkins that match the tablecloth are in bee-adorned napkin rings. I'm sensing a theme. There is a blue pottery jug in the middle of the table, full of beautiful flowers. There is a real bee buzzing around in the blooms, which makes me smile. Lucy tells me that Meredith brought the flowers, so maybe it is okay to bring coals to Newcastle after all.

I can't see Alex in the garden; maybe he is in the Zen sanctuary, meditating. I imagine sitting next to him, cross-legged on a tatami mat, eyes closed, the sound of our breathing punctuated by birdsong. Then I hear Meredith's voice. "I just love delphiniums, don't you?" and the mood is shattered. I wouldn't know a delphinium if I fell into a bed of them.

Meredith climbs the steps, her arms full of long-stemmed, intensely blue flowers the exact color of Alex's eyes. Alex and Nori are standing at the bottom of the steps, deep in conversation. Meredith says, "Oh, hi, Harry," as if she's surprised—and not particularly pleased—to see me. "Lucy, can you show me where to find a vase for these?"

Lucy follows her obediently into the house. Clearly I'm not Meredith's favorite half-sister. And she's not mine. I'm still not exactly sure why.

"If the bees die, we die," Nori is saying to Alex. "It's that simple. No pollination, no plants. No plants, no life as we know it."

Alex nods and then looks up at me and smiles. "Hey, Harry," he says. "You should see the garden." He turns to Nori. "Can I show her around? While I still remember all the stuff you told us?"

"Sure," Nori says. "Shoes off in the sanctuary though." She frowns at my flip-flops, as if they are stilettos.

"We'll be careful," Alex says.

Nori nods and heads into the house, leaving me alone with Alex.

"So. Quite the place, hey?" he says.

I nod and go down the stairs into the garden, where Alex is standing by a bush covered in small white blooms—obviously the source of Lucy's garland.

"Smell this," he says, and I lean over and inhale. It's incredible.

"Mock orange," he says, as I continue to breathe in the intoxicating citrus-y scent.

"My mom wears perfume that smells like this," I say. "I love it, even though most perfume makes me sneeze."

Alex laughs and heads down a path made of crushed white shells. "Nori collected these shells, and Angela crushed them in a walking meditation," he tells me.

"They're from beaches all over the world. She's been collecting them for years. Still does."

The shells crunch softly as we walk over them. "Won't they eventually turn to dust or sand or something?" I ask.

Alex shrugs. "Apparently she keeps adding shells to the paths, and Angela keeps crushing them. Friends collect them for her too. She says the path is a metaphor for life."

The shell path ends at a small wooden bridge that arches over an undulating stream of river rocks and leads to a tiny cedar hut set in a wide carpet of bright-green moss. There are stone benches outside the hut, one on each side of the open doorway. I slip off my flip-flops, and Alex slides his feet out of his deck shoes. His feet are narrow and tan, his nails trimmed. Guys' feet can be gross; his are not. The hair on his legs is fine and golden. There is a large ugly scar above his left knee. Inside the hut, the floor is covered with straw mats, just as I had imagined. A low altar holds one white pillar candle, a statue of the Buddha and a single white orchid in a green pot. Two round red pillows face the altar. No glass in the windows; no door. It's beautiful but kind of stark. I can't imagine wanting to meditate out here during a Seattle winter. But then again, I can't imagine wanting to meditate at all.

As if reading my thoughts, Alex says, "Nori told me that Angela only uses this in good weather. She has another meditation space inside."

We go back across the bridge and Alex points out various plants as we wander through the garden:

butterfly bush, lady's-mantle, delphinium, phlox, lavender. It occurs to me that he may be trying to impress me, and since I don't know much about plants, it kind of works. Eventually he stops playing botanist—I think he's run out of plant names—but I don't mind; the garden seems to welcome silence. I think about my mom, trying to meditate in her cluttered office. I wonder how she feels, if she's jealous of Angela and Nori with their beautiful house and garden, their two incomes and two kids, their loving relationship. Does she have regrets? Does she wish this were her life?

"Was your mom ever married?" Alex asks as we approach the house. It's starting to freak me out a bit— the way he always seems to know what I'm thinking.

"Nope," I say. "Not her thing, I guess. She left home really young, and Verna took her in. She went to school for years and now she works super hard. Not much time for a relationship. At least, that's what she tells me."

"Verna?"

I've forgotten that Alex hasn't met Verna, but I'm surprised Meredith hasn't told him about coming to the salon.

"She's my grandmother. Not by blood—I've never met my real grandparents—but she helped raise me. She's here for dinner too. It's a regular family reunion."

"Or irregular," Alex says.

I laugh, and we climb the stairs to the deck just as Lucy comes out of the house with Meredith.

"Our moms are bonding like crazy," Lucy says. "Turns out your mom teaches with one of Angela's friends. It's like old home week in there, isn't it, Meredith? Verna and Nori are setting up the Scrabble board for after dinner. Angela hates games. She wouldn't even play Uno with us when we were little. She claims games *encourage a negative spirit of competitiveness*. Nori disagrees."

"Verna's a pretty cutthroat Scrabble player," I say. "She may look like a sweet old lady, but she will block your triple word score in a heartbeat."

Alex laughs, and Meredith's thin lips stretch over her little teeth. Tonight she's wearing a pink-and-white-checked shirtdress with a wide pink belt. Demure but not dowdy. Her hair is more gamine than spiky tonight. What is it about her that rubs me the wrong way, apart from the fact that she always seems to be wearing a costume? Retro movie star. Girl next door. It all seems so calculated. Or maybe she's just more interested in fashion than I am. Almost everyone is.

By the time we've finished the salmon and new potatoes and salad, I've figured out another thing that bugs me: Meredith is an expert on everything we talk about. She danced professionally, she volunteered at a shelter for at-risk youth, she worked on an organic farm one summer, she writes poetry, she won a competition for young chefs. She even took woodworking in high school because *home ec was so lame*. She built bookcases for the school library and did fundraising for a school in Africa. I get tired just listening to her, but I can't exactly compete, although I do agree about home ec. And everyone else seems impressed.

When Mom asks her where the shelter was, Meredith says, "Boise."

"Oh, you must have been at Your Place," Mom says. "A friend of mine's the director. I didn't think they had peer volunteers."

"It's a new program," Meredith says, and before Mom can ask her anything else, Angela brings in Verna's cake, which is so delicious that all conversation stops for a while. Meredith doesn't eat much cake—she asks for "just a sliver"—but I can see her darting glances at Mom. Her expression is odd—not exactly fearful but certainly wary, which is weird. Mom's tough but hardly threatening. At the first opportunity, Meredith excuses herself from the table and goes inside. When she comes back, she sits at the top of the stairs, her back to the rest of us, gazing into the garden. Mom looks thoughtful, as if she's working through an interesting problem.

When Verna and Nori go inside to play Scrabble, Angela starts to clear the table. Meredith jumps up to help, but Angela is firm—Lucy can help, but guests cannot.

Mom wanders out into the garden, leaving Meredith, Alex and me on the deck.

"This is the most peaceful place I've ever been," Meredith says. "Lucy is so lucky."

I nod. I want to ask her what her home in Montana was like, but she is already talking to Alex about getting a community-garden plot and growing all their own vegetables.

"Do you have a garden?" she asks me.

"Not like this one," I say. "Tiny front lawn with a few flower beds. Brick patio in the back. A few planters. Gardening's not really Mom's thing."

"Maybe you could garden in Harry's front yard," Alex says to Meredith.

I can't tell whether he's joking. I hope so. I don't know what to say, so I ask him if we're still on for a dog walk the next day. Meredith glares at Alex when he says yes.

"We should get going," she says to him.

"We can drive you home," I say. "Mom won't mind. Unless you live in Edmonds or something. But we'll have to wait for Nori and Verna to finish their game."

"We'll take the bus," Meredith says. "We have to work tomorrow. Let's go, Alex."

Alex says, "I'd like to stay awhile," and Meredith looks as if she's been slapped. Her face reddens.

"Suit yourself," she says. "I'm leaving."

She get up and stalks into the house; Alex follows her. I stay behind on the deck. When Mom comes in from the garden, she raises her eyebrows and asks, "Where is everybody?"

"Nori and Verna are playing Scrabble, Angela and Lucy are doing the dishes, and Meredith and Alex are arguing over whether to take the bus or wait for a ride."

"I'm happy to give them a ride home," she says. "Unless they live in Edmonds."

I laugh. "That's what I said. Why is it we always say Edmonds is too far to go?"

"Because it is," she says. "Alex seems like a lovely person."

I nod. "Except for being Meredith's bitch." The words pop out of my mouth like jawbreakers from a gumball machine.

Mom's eyebrows go up again. "They're obviously very close," she says. "Have they been friends a long time?"

"Since they were little kids."

Mom nods. "Hard to get in the middle of that, I would imagine."

"She hates me," I say.

"I'm sure she doesn't hate you, Harry. Maybe she feels threatened by you—it's pretty clear that Alex likes you."

I shrug and feel myself blushing. "Maybe."

Mom laughs. "Maybe? It's to his credit that he wants to be a good friend to Meredith too."

"Not if he never stands up for himself."

"Give it some time," Mom says. "You only just met. Maybe if she understands that you won't take him away from her…"

I'm about to say, *But I'd sort of like to* when Alex appears on the porch.

"We're going to take the bus. Don't want to inconvenience anyone. See you tomorrow, Harry," he says. "Nice to meet you, Della."

"You too, Alex," Mom says.

I'm suddenly so upset, all I can bring myself to say is "Bye." Maybe I should just go back to the café and flirt with Nate. It would be so much simpler.

On the drive home, I sit in the backseat and listen to Mom and Verna dissect the evening: the house (gorgeous, but the taxes must be huge), the food (delicious, especially the cake), the garden (wonderful, but a lot of work), Angela and Nori (delightful and tough, respectively), Lucy (cute and talented). When they get to Alex and Meredith, there's a long pause before Verna declares, "He's a peach, but I'm not sure about her. I can't quite put my finger on it."

"I think Harry would agree with you about that," Mom says, glancing at me in the rearview mirror.

"There's something peculiar about her," Verna continues. "I thought so when she came to the salon. And before you start lecturing me about being judgmental, Della, tell me you don't agree. I saw the look on your face when she was talking about that shelter in Boise. Do you think she ever worked there?"

Mom sighs. "No, I don't. The woman who runs the shelter is very outspoken about peer volunteers.

She's against them, for various reasons. But why would Meredith lie? That's what puzzles me."

Verna says, "Who knows? But she's troubled, that's for sure."

"But still, why lie?" I lean forward and ask. "Because she wants people to like her?"

"Maybe the reality of her life is too difficult," Mom says. "Didn't you say she's estranged from her family? And she's not having any success finding her donor?"

"Do you always have to play sociologist?" I ask. "Maybe she's just a shitty person. End of story."

"It's never the end of the story," Mom says. "You know better than that, Harry."

"So nobody's a jerk for no reason?"

"Not usually," Mom says.

"That's such bullshit."

"I'm not going to argue with you, Harry."

"Yeah, you're the one with the PhD. I forgot for a minute."

"Stop it, you two," Verna says. "We don't know Meredith well enough yet to know what motivates her. But I hope Angela and Nori keep an eye on Lucy. She's clearly very impressionable."

Mom nods. "I agree. But Meredith is Harry's half-sister too, and I think we need to give her the benefit of the doubt. For now."

"Are we even sure she's my half-sister?" I say. "She doesn't look anything like me or Lucy or Ben or Adam."

"Just because you don't like her doesn't mean you're not related," Mom says.

Even so, I wonder how you go about testing DNA. It looks so easy on TV: a hair here, a fingernail clipping there. I pull out my phone and Google *DNA sibling test*. Turns out that for two hundred dollars, I could find out whether Meredith really is my half-sibling. I wouldn't even need a cheek swab (which is the preferred method). DNA can be extracted from all sorts of gross things: used chewing gum, Band-Aids, dental floss, toothpicks. Of course, it would be a total invasion of her privacy, but at this point I'm not sure I care.

EIGHT

I'M AT THE SALON, sweeping up hair, when I get a text from Alex: **Have to cancel walk with Churchill. Something came up. Sorry. Talk soon.**

"Shit!"

"Language," Verna says, even though there are no clients in the shop.

"Sorry," I say. "Alex canceled our date."

"Your date?"

"Yeah. Dog walking. So romantic, right?"

Verna laughs. "Could be, I guess. Depends on the dog. And the boy. But there's no point getting upset. He probably had to work. He told me last night that his shifts are unpredictable. And he seems very responsible. Maybe he's saving up to take you somewhere nice. Ever think of that?"

I shake my head. She may be right. Of course he can't pass up a shift. He pays rent somewhere, buys his own food, pays bills. I have no idea what that's like. But why wouldn't he just say he had to work?

I text back. **No problem. Another time.**

Then I text Lucy. **Wanna hang out this afternoon?**

I don't hear back immediately—maybe she's in a dance class—and the salon gets busy. By the time it slows down, around one, she still hasn't responded, so I head home for lunch and an afternoon of transcribing. I have the house to myself, which I usually like, but today I can't settle to anything. The case file I'm working on doesn't hold my attention. Or maybe I just don't want to think about all the unhappiness in the world. I don't know how Mom does it. She seems to have endless compassion for the girls she interviews. Mine is starting to wear thin already. I only get halfway through an interview with Jessica, a girl from a rich family who just wants to get high and piss off her parents, both of which she does with great efficiency. Until they kick her out. Her ambition is to set herself up as a high-end call girl (she has the right wardrobe and really likes rich older men—hello, daddy issues). In the meantime, she's crashing wherever she can find a guy to take her in. Lots of guys are happy to do so. I don't like her. She sounds manipulative and shallow, not like the other girls in the study.

I try to read a novel Mom thought I would like— something about a woman doctor who goes to the Amazon—but I fall asleep reading it. My phone pings at about five o'clock. Lucy.

Just got your text. Went to EMP with M & A. It was amazing. Thought you had to work.

I love the Experience Music Project, even if it is kind of touristy. Mom took Byron and me there for my birthday when I turned twelve. Then we went for lunch at the Space Needle. Also super touristy, but when you're twelve, you don't care. You just want the Lunar Orbit sundae. Byron and I went to EMP a lot after that, sometimes just to mess around in the sound booths, making up dumb songs and pretending we were rock stars. I haven't been for a while. I would have loved to go. It takes a minute for me to wake up enough to realize that someone—I can guess who—told Lucy I couldn't go with them. And that Alex has chosen my sisters over me. It also occurs to me that there's no point taking it out on Lucy.

I text back, **Hope the Hendrix show was still on. It's awesome!**

Before I can hit *Send*, my phone rings. I look at the screen—Alex's number. I dismiss the call, send my message to Lucy and shut my phone off. I need to think. Mom's motto is When in doubt, write it out. She believes that most problems can be solved, or at least understood, by working through them on a piece of paper. Not on a computer. You have to use lined yellow legal paper and a pen or it won't work. It has something to do with the physical act of writing and how that affects your brain.

I have watched her do it many times. Usually wine is involved, and swearing. Maybe now is the time to try it myself. Minus the wine.

I grab some paper and a pen and sit at the kitchen table. The only thing I can think of writing is a chronology of events, followed by a list of things I know about Alex and Meredith. I leave Lucy out of the equation—I don't have a problem with her. And I'm not really sure what my problem with Meredith and Alex is.

When Mom comes home an hour later, I'm still sitting at the table. I have about five pages of scribbled notes, which I'm reading over. I think Mom's method may be working, because I'm beginning to put some things together.

Things I know about Alex:

- *He met Meredith in Montana, when he moved there from Texas in first grade.*
- *He's 18.*
- *He doesn't talk about his family.*
- *He works at a restaurant and volunteers at an animal shelter.*
- *He always wears gray plaid shorts, button shirts, Vans.*
- *His voice is quite soft. He laughs easily.*
- *He likes me (or at least I thought he did).*
- *He does whatever Meredith wants.*

Things I don't know:

- *His last name.*
- *Where he lives.*
- *Where he works.*
- *Why he likes Meredith so much.*

Things I know about Meredith:

- *Her last name is Leatherby.*
- *She comes from Missoula, Montana.*
- *She says she has danced in Denver and worked at a shelter in Boise.*
- *Meredith is estranged from her parents and wants to find her "father."*
- *Her clothes look like costumes.*
- *She is manipulative (Lucy's hair) and super sensitive (arm grabbing).*

Things I don't know:

- *Where she lives.*
- *Where she worked on an organic farm.*
- *How she can have done all the things she says she's done.*
- *Why she hates me.*
- *Why she has such a hold on Alex.*

Questions:

- *Is Meredith a liar?*
- *What will I do if (when) I find out she is? Is it important to find out why she's lying (if she is)?*
- *Should I tell Lucy what I'm doing? Should I tell Mom? Should I call Alex back?*

"You okay, Harry?" Mom asks as she pours herself a glass of wine. "You were sighing."

"I was?"

She sits at the table across from me. My notes are still in front of me. She can probably read upside down, but she doesn't seem to be trying to. All she says is, "If you ever want to talk…"

"I know where to find you," I say. And we both laugh. We've been saying that for years. She knows I'll talk when I'm ready. This time, I'm not so sure I'll ever be ready. I doubt whether she'd approve of my plan to spy on Meredith.

"I did some transcribing today," I say. "Really didn't like the girl. Jessica."

Mom nods. "She's a tough one, I'll admit. Not exactly a kindred spirit. But still homeless."

"If you count shacking up with assholes as homeless."

"I do. You may not approve of her coping mechanisms, but she still deserves my attention. And a proper home."

"But she's not the same as the other girls," I say. "Like Annabeth. She's got real talent, and she's so smart and optimistic, but her life is really hard. Jessica just wants to party and have someone else pay for it."

"You're awfully judgmental today. What's going on? I thought you were seeing Alex."

"He bailed."

"That's disappointing."

"He and Lucy and Meredith went to EMP. Without me."

"Ouch."

"Big ouch."

"Have you talked to him?"

I shake my head. "He called. I didn't answer."

"Maybe you should give him a chance to explain." Mom takes a sip of wine and then gets to her feet. "I picked up some stuff for burgers. Could you fire up the barbecue? And organize the fixings?"

"Sure." I take my notes to my room and turn on my phone. Alex has called three times and left one voice mail. The voice mail is in his dopey Churchill voice. "That idiot Alex canceled today, and I missed you. Can you come tomorrow? I want to lick your face. I want to hear you whistle. I want to sniff some other dogs' butts. Can you bring treats? Alex sometimes forgets. He says he's very sorry about today. He says wires got crossed, whatever that means. Maybe wires are like leashes. I hate leashes, especially if they get crossed. I'll be waiting at the bus stop at two o'clock. Drooling."

I laugh in spite of myself. Maybe Mom's right—I should give him a chance to explain. Before I go downstairs to help with dinner, I text Alex. **Hi, Churchill. See you tomorrow. I missed you too.**

After dinner, Mom and I watch a great documentary about backup singers (which makes me think about Annabeth and all the opportunities she'll probably never have), and then I head up to my room to start my research. The Leatherbys of Missoula, Montana, are ridiculously easy to find. I am deeply grateful that Meredith's last name isn't Smith or Jones. In five minutes I have the address and phone number of a Barbara Leatherby, who I assume is Meredith's mom. I could phone her right now if I felt like it, but I'm not sure what I'd say. *Hi, my name is Harriet. Could you please confirm that your daughter is a pathological liar?* I dig a little deeper. There's a Mark Leatherby in Missoula as well. I note his address and phone number too.

I put Barbara's address into Google Street View. Her house is a large gray-and-white rancher with a two-car garage, a big yellowing lawn and beds of what look like roses lining the walkway. There's a beige sedan in the garage. Next door is an almost identical house, minus the roses. Ditto across the street. Bland and boring, not at all what I'd expected. For some reason, I'd pictured Meredith living in a crappy trailer park, with a battered pickup truck out front and beer cans littering the yard. No way had I imagined Suburbia, USA. With roses, no less.

Mark Leatherby, whoever he is, lives in a heritage house on the other side of town. Beautiful paint job. Late-model Subaru Outback in the driveway. So far, so good.

I'm starting to feel all Harriet the Spy, except that my spying will have to be done online. I wish I could go to Missoula, but it's an eight-hour drive and no way would Mom let me go there on my own. Especially if I told her why I was going. Before I go to bed, I make a to-do list of all the things I need to check out: Missoula newspapers, Denver dance companies, that shelter in Boise.

I'm in bed, reading an online article about dog training, when my phone pings.

I miss you. B.

Even a few weeks ago, a text like that from Byron would have destroyed me. And for sure I would have seriously considered texting him back. Right after he left, my sadness clawed at me, devouring me, day by lonely day. Since I met Lucy, I've only felt the occasional twinge, like when you bite the inside of your cheek. Painful for a minute but forgotten almost right away. I do miss him but not the way I did before. Mostly I wish I could talk to him about everything that's going on. I wonder what he'd think about my new siblings, about Alex. And does it make me shallow or fickle that I look at his text and wish the *B* was an *A*? I turn my phone off, roll over and go to sleep.

The next day when I'm getting ready to meet Alex, I try not to worry too much about what I'm wearing. White shorts, a plain blue T-shirt, runners. Hair in a French braid. No makeup. Well, mascara, but that hardly counts. I always wear mascara. I want Alex to see me as I really am: no costumes, no games. Just plain old level-headed Harry.

But when I'm on the bus to the shelter, I start to panic. My T-shirt has stains under the arms. My shorts are frayed. I've had these runners since ninth grade. What was I thinking? But then, there he is, a big grin on his face as I step off the bus. And suddenly I'm sure he doesn't care what I'm wearing, any more than I care that he's got on the same old gray shorts, wrinkled shirt and beat-up shoes. Churchill is at his side, drooling, as promised.

As soon as I'm off the bus, Churchill starts dancing around me, pulling hard on the leash and barking like crazy.

"You know I brought treats, don't you, buddy?" I say. "You'll have to sit."

He continues to prance, and I say "Sit!" in a stern voice. Miraculously, he obeys, and I reward him with a biscuit from my pocket.

"He won't always sit for me," Alex says. "You clearly have the magic touch."

"And the treats. Treats are key."

We set out for the dog park, Churchill straining on the leash. Alex keeps trying to get him to heel, but Churchill keeps pulling.

"Let me try," I say, taking the leash from Alex, who looks skeptical.

"He's really strong," he says.

"So am I."

I make Churchill sit again, reward him with a treat and then, when we start walking, step in front of him every time he starts to pull. We make slow progress, but after a couple of blocks he's pulling less and less.

"Where did you learn that?" Alex asks. "You're like the Dog Whisperer."

"Hardly," I say. "Just experienced. I walk dogs in my neighborhood. Not all of them come to me well trained. So I learned a few tricks."

"Very impressive," Alex says. "A girl who does her research. I like that."

"You have no idea. I put footnotes in my book reports in third grade. It was so obnoxious. That's what being raised by an academic will do to you."

And you wouldn't like it if you knew what else I was researching, I think. We reach the park, and I let Churchill off the leash. As he bounds away, Alex says, "I'm sorry about yesterday. Things got...complicated. Meredith was really upset about something. She left work and asked me to meet her, but by the time I got there, she'd made plans with Lucy."

"So you all went to EMP," I say, trying to keep an accusatory tone out of my voice.

He nods. "I'm sorry. I messed up. I should have called you."

"What was Meredith so upset about?" I ask.

"I'm not sure. Whatever it was, she got over it before I got there. She must have talked to Lucy or something."

I watch Churchill for a few minutes. If you ever wanted a demonstration of the word *gamboling*, all you'd have to do is watch Churchill playing with his doggy friends. I envied him. The world could use more gamboling and less stressing. More treats and fewer commands. I take a deep breath and say, "Do you always do whatever Meredith wants?"

Silence.

Someone calls their dog—"Scout! Get over here! Scout!"—and a border collie streaks across the park.

When Alex finally replies, his voice is stiff and formal. "I said I was sorry. But Meredith is my best friend. You have no idea the stuff she's done for me. Don't you have a friend like that?"

He turns toward me and looks steadily into my eyes. He doesn't look angry, just serious. I look away. I can't tell him about Byron, my best friend turned boyfriend turned...nothing. Byron, who misses me. Byron, who would do whatever I wanted—except stay.

"Sort of," I say. I turn and start walking back to the bus stop.

Alex says, "Don't go, Harriet. Please. You haven't taught me to whistle yet. And Churchill could always use some more leash training."

"That's true," I say, and I know there is nothing I want more than to stay.

By the time I get home, it's almost dark. Alex and I have spent almost eight hours together, first at the park with Churchill (who earned a lot of treats by learning to roll over) and then at a sushi bar Gwen and I go to a lot. I love sushi, so I was able to show off a bit, ordering stuff Alex had never had. Maybe Missoula doesn't have a lot of sushi restaurants. Spicy squid salad, shumai, drunk clams. After that we got gelato at Gelatiamo (chocolate chili/coconut for me, hazelnut/pistachio for Alex) and walked for ages, ending up at Myrtle Edwards Park, where we sat on a bench while the sun set. We talked a lot, but not about anything important. Sometimes we were silent, and it didn't feel awkward at all. When we finally said goodbye at my bus stop, I was exhausted but wired. The combination of sunshine, sushi, sugar and happiness made me bolder than I usually am. The bus pulled up, and I kissed Alex on the mouth—really fast but hard, no tongue. I could taste the pistachios on his lips. Delicious. He looked startled, but he didn't pull away or wipe his mouth afterward.

I laughed and said, "Thanks for the great day" and jumped onto the bus.

Now I can't sleep, so I get up and continue researching the Leatherbys of Missoula, Montana.

NINE

THERE ARE A LOT of Leatherbys in England, an ice-cream parlor called Leatherby's in California, and the Leatherby Libraries are part of some university in California. And that's just on the first page. Google can be overwhelming sometimes, so I decide to try my luck on Facebook. Lots of my friends' parents have Facebook pages. My friends mock their moms' posts or their dads' profile shots and bitch about how their parents are tracking their every move. My mom doesn't have a page, and I doubt she's ever looked at mine. She says she doesn't have time for Facebook, and she thinks selfies are evidence of the downfall of civilization. Now I'm hoping that Barbara Leatherby has embraced social media. Maybe she even has a Twitter handle.

I type her name into the Find Friends space and, lo and behold, there she is. Barbara Jean Leatherby of

Missoula, Montana. Blond, tanned, fiftyish. Sporty-looking—not like Meredith at all. Her cover picture is a rose, which makes sense. I can't see much else without friending her, but I can see where she works (at the University of Montana), her relationship status (*It's complicated*) and where she went to school (UC Berkeley).

Next I search for Mark Leatherby. He is about Barbara's age, maybe a bit older. Clearly not Meredith's brother. I click on his profile. He's dark-haired and thin-faced, with a goatee and wire-framed glasses. His cover picture is a photo of two dogs—one looks like an overgrown fox, the other is some kind of terrier. Mark also works at the university and has a complicated relationship. Who doesn't? And, like Barbara's, his privacy settings don't allow me to see his friends or his posts.

I wonder if Alex has a Facebook profile, but since I still don't know his last name, it's impossible to search for him. I make a mental note to work it naturally into the conversation the next time I see him. My mind wanders a bit, replaying our day together, especially the kiss, wondering if he's as wide awake as I am. When I look for Meredith Leatherby on Facebook, all I find is her "looking for daddy" page, so I move on to the *Missoulian* newspaper, type the name Leatherby into the Search field and hope for the best.

When the screen fills with citations, I'm excited—until I realize there's a local tack shop named Leatherby's in Missoula. Apparently it has the best selection of cowboy boots in Montana. I've always wanted cowboy boots. Red ones. Another reason to go to Missoula. Finally I come across a Barbara Leatherby, manager of the bookstore at the university. She's excited about a famous Montana author who's going to do an event at the store. Interesting, but not much help. Barbara pops up again in an article about a pottery show at a local community center. There's a picture of her smiling and holding up a beautiful vase. She is quoted as saying that "making pottery is a meditation for me, an opportunity to be with my own thoughts."

Barbara shows up a few more times, but there's no sign of Mark until I find an obituary from 1999 that lists him as the son of the dearly departed Jack Leatherby, a retired dentist. Next to Mark's name is Barbara's, in parentheses, which means they are (or were) husband and wife. Holy shit! I get up and pace my room. In 1999, Meredith would have been what? Two or three? I read the entire obituary. Mark is the only child of Jack and his deceased wife, Rose. Jack's beloved grandchildren are listed as Jackson, Elizabeth and Meredith. I find the birth announcements for all three kids—Jackson and Elizabeth are twins, three years older than Meredith. Parents: Mark and Barbara Leatherby.

I shut down the computer, get back into bed and try to force my tired brain to make sense of what I've discovered. Meredith has two siblings (possibly not biological). Her parents are separated or maybe divorced.

Her grandfather was a dentist. I fall asleep wondering whether Alex has secrets too.

The next day I work in the salon, finish my transcription of Jessica's interview (I still don't like her) and clean the house, which Mom pays me to do once a week. I don't hear from Alex, but I assume he's working, although I still don't know where. Verna comes over for dinner, and afterward she beats us both at Scrabble, since she seems to have memorized the latest edition of the *Official Scrabble Dictionary*. She plays *chillax* and *bromance* and *qajaq*, which she puts on a triple word score; Mom and I don't stand a chance. When the game is over, I say goodnight and go upstairs to check out the *Missoula Independent*.

The *Independent* is a community newspaper, full of stories about local people and events. Almost right away, I find an article about Elizabeth Leatherby's move to Denver to dance in the company that Meredith told us she belonged to. The accompanying photograph shows a small, lithe blond girl in mid-leap. My heart starts to race; this is the first evidence I have found that confirms my suspicions about Meredith. Then I find a picture of some volunteers at an organic farm. Second from the left, leaning on a fence, grinning, is Jackson Leatherby. He looks like his father—dark-haired and wiry, with glasses and a scruffy beard. Next to him, a beautiful girl with long, wildly curly hair is gazing up at him adoringly. No wonder he looks so happy. Organic veggies and love are a potent combo.

Jackson and Elizabeth show up in older articles as well. When they graduated from Big Sky High, they were co-valedictorians. They formed a hiking group in high school called the Jumbotrons, named after nearby Mount Jumbo, their favorite place to hike. How cool is it to live near a mountain named after a Disney elephant? They also took part in the annual community weed-pulls on Mount Jumbo. I bet their parents were proud.

There's no mention of Meredith at all until I come across a short article about her Little League team, which played in the Little League World Series when Meredith was twelve. She was the star shortstop. And there she is in the team photo. Front and center, smirking, lips tight. Behind her, a tall girl with curly blond hair smiles broadly at the camera. I scan the names under the picture: the tall girl's name is Danielle Larson, and she looks exactly like Alex.

Alex must have a twin sister. Weird that he hasn't mentioned her. Mind you, he hasn't told me anything about his family. And I haven't asked.

I wake up with a brutal headache and call Verna to tell her I can't help in the salon today. Then I text Mom that

I'm sick and going back to sleep. No way I can face the Sunday ladies today. I stay in bed until I hear the front door shut and the car start. When I go downstairs, a note on the kitchen table says, *Feel better, Harry. Call if you need anything.* I take an Advil, make some toast and stare out the window as I eat it.

My phone pings as I'm putting my dishes in the dishwasher.

The text from Lucy says, **Wanna hang out 2day?**

I text back, **Can't. Sick. Sorry.**

Bummer.

Yeah. Going back to sleep. Call you later.

She responds with an emoticon of a toilet and **lol!**

I smile and send her a happy face in a surgical mask. I go back to sleep for a couple of hours, and when I wake up my headache is almost gone. I open up the *Missoula Independent* again and search for Alex Larson. Nothing. I google *Larson + Missoula*. Not surprisingly, there are pages of Larsons. A needle in a haystack, as Verna would say. I go back to my best lead—Barbara Leatherby. I consider messaging her on Facebook, but it would be the longest message ever, and who knows if she's even on Facebook very often. I have her home phone number. I can imagine her sitting with a cup of tea on her front porch, reading a novel, admiring her roses. Do I want to mess with that? Do I have any choice?

Of course I do. Mom has been hammering it into my head since birth—maybe even in the womb. I imagine her stroking her big belly, crooning into her navel, *You always have choices, little one. Always.* So I know I can shut it all down right now. Let the chips fall et cetera, et cetera. But do I want to? No. What's the worst that can happen? Barbara hangs up on me. Or she could freak out—that's always a possibility. Or tell me stuff I don't want to hear. Another thing Verna always says: *Don't ask the question if you're not prepared for the answer.* Am I prepared? I'm not sure. All I know is I'll go nuts if I don't do something.

I pick up the phone, take a deep breath and dial Barbara's number. I don't have a script or even a plan. When she answers, I simply say, "My name is Harriet Jacobs. I'm calling from Seattle, and I'd like to talk to you about your daughter Meredith."

She gasps. "What? Who is this?"

"My name is Harriet Jacobs," I repeat. "Meredith is in Seattle. She contacted me through the DSR—the Donor Sibling—"

"I know what it is," she says. "Is Merry all right?"

Merry? She calls her Merry? I can't put that together with the girl I know, who is the opposite of merry.

"Um, I think so."

Barbara is silent for a moment, and then she asks, "Do you Skype?"

I nod but say "Yes" when I remember she can't see me.

"Let's do that, then. What's your Skype name? I'll be in touch within the hour." She's all business now, the quaver in her voice gone.

"Harrietthespy," I say. Then I realize how creepy that must sound, given what I've been doing. "After the book, you know? All one word."

"I'll call you soon, Harriet," she says.

Fifty-seven long minutes later, she's on my screen, sitting exactly where I had imagined her—on a white wicker settee on her porch. She looks like her Facebook picture, only not smiling. Next to her is Mark Leatherby. Also not smiling.

"Hi," I say.

"Hello," Barbara says. "This is Mark, Merry's father. But you probably already know that."

I'm not sure what to say, so I opt for the truth. "I found you both on Facebook. And there was some stuff in the Montana newspapers too."

"Why were you looking for us? Is Merry in trouble?" Barbara says. Still no smile.

"Not that I know of," I say. "Her friend Alex is here too. They seem…fine."

Mark nods. "I'm not surprised they're together. They've been friends since they met at T-ball. Thick as thieves."

I nod. "His sister must miss him," I say. "Being twins and all."

Barbara and Mark look puzzled. "Sister?" Mark says. "Alex doesn't have a sister. Just an older brother."

"But I saw her picture. She was on the Little League team with Meredith. Danielle Larson."

A look passes between Mark and Barbara that is hard to interpret. Mark gives a small shrug, and Barbara says, "You need to talk to Alex about that. We appreciate the call, Harriet, but I'm not sure what more we can tell you. Merry has made it clear she wants nothing to do with us. And we don't feel comfortable talking to a stranger about her."

Mark adds, "But please call us again if something is wrong—with Merry or Alex. If they need our help."

"Okay," I mumble. "Thanks for talking to me. Bye."

I close the connection and lie down on my bed.

When I shut my eyes, all I can see is Danielle Larson in her baseball uniform. I sit up and open the *Missoulian* again, searching for birth notices. I finally find it. *Danielle Margaret Larson, born April 12, 1997, to Darrell and Donna Larson. Big brother Donnie is thrilled. Praise Jesus.* Mark was right. No twin sister. Just Danielle. I open up the Little League article again and stare at the picture of Danielle Larson. If it were in color, I'm sure her eyes would be lapis blue.

Back to Google, this time searching for Darrell and Donna Larson. It only takes a few minutes to find their address and phone number. Before I can think better of it, I dial the number. A woman answers. She sounds as if she's smoked a pack a day for the last fifty years.

I ask, "Is Danielle there?" and there is such a long silence, I think she's hung up.

"Who wants to know?" she finally says.

"Um, I'm doing a piece for the *Missoulian* on, uh…" I'm drawing a blank, but she fills it in for me.

"On how a good Christian family can produce a monster? You're not the first to ask." She laughs—or at least I think it's a laugh. It sounds like shears cutting through sheet metal. "Danielle's dead to me," she continues. "You put that in your paper. Oh, I know she calls herself Alex now. I know she calls herself a man. A man! That girl is no more a man than I am! I did what I could—raised her right. But she was tainted, and nothing we did changed that. And that's all I have to say."

She hangs up, and all I can think is, Alex is a girl. Even though he's not. I wish I'd never gone looking for information about Meredith. I wish I'd just left well enough alone. I don't care anymore if she's my half-sister or a serial killer or both. All I care about is who Alex is, and whether he was ever going to tell me.

My heart is racing, and I can feel beads of sweat forming along my hairline. My mouth is dry. Alex was born a girl. A girl named Danielle. He's a boy now, so that means he's transgender. I know about the difference between sexual orientation and gender identity. A trans girl named Sabrina came to our school last year, and she got hassled by a few idiots, who were suspended.

Our school's Gay-Straight Alliance did a presentation about being trans at an assembly. It was the first time I heard the expression "Sex is what's between your legs. Gender is what's between your ears." But right now it's hard not to think about what is (or isn't) between Alex's legs.

As far as I can tell, Alex likes girls. I like boys. No problem. In theory, it sounds straightforward— reasonable, even—but the reality is something else. I've never even slept with a guy *with* a dick. Maybe it's better that I have no basis for comparison. But the questions just keep coming: Does Alex take hormones? Has he had surgery? What would it be like to make out with someone who has breasts and a vagina? And does wanting to make me a lesbian? I know it doesn't, but I still ask myself the question.

I lie down again and toss and turn, sweating, flailing, pummeling the pillow. Nothing helps. The only way I can answer my questions is to talk to Alex. And right now, I'm too scared.

My phone rings in the early afternoon. Lucy. I don't have the energy for her right now. And I'm afraid I might repeat what I found out about Alex and Meredith, which I don't want to do. Not yet anyway. I'd like Lucy to think well of me for as long as possible. Maybe if we'd grown up together, I wouldn't worry about disappointing her. I've seen my friends treat their siblings like shit and it doesn't seem to damage their relationships. This seems way more fragile.

A couple of minutes later, there's a text message from her: **Our donor contacted Meredith!!!!!!!!!!**

Followed by one from Alex: **I need to see you.**

And one from Byron: **I really miss you. I'm thinking of coming home.**

As Verna says, it never rains but it pours.

TEN

ROCK AND A HARD PLACE. *Devil and the deep blue sea.* I lie on the couch and try to think of all the ways Verna would describe my situation. I get stuck on *Damned if you do, damned if you don't.*

I jump when the phone rings. It's Mom, checking in. I tell her the (partial) truth: I'm lying on the couch and I don't feel very well. She says she'll pick me up a variety pack of Rachel's Ginger Beer, which is my favorite drink in the world, sick or not. A bottle of RGB—any flavor—makes everything better. I feel guilty when I thank her. Being deceitful is so exhausting. I wonder how Meredith does it.

I turn my phone off and go for a walk with one of my favorite dogs, a calm, intelligent sweetheart named Ketch. My thoughts feel like out-of-control bumper cars, but I slow them down with some music—Fox Glove,

Halsey, St. Vincent. I walk for miles, enjoying the thudding of my feet on the pavement, the slight breeze off the Sound. For a while I almost forget about half-sisters and donor dads and probably-trans boys. Almost.

When I get back, there are seven messages on my phone. Two each from Lucy, Alex and Byron. One from Meredith. They all say basically the same thing: *Where the hell are you???*

I ignore everyone but Alex. All that donor drama can wait. And Byron? A month ago I would have been ecstatic if he said he was coming home. Now I just don't know. It's not like I can talk to him about Alex. But part of me really wants to ask if we can be friends again. I can't face that right now. It's not like he's turning up tomorrow.

I text Alex: **What's up?**

He texts right back: **I'd like to see you again.**

When?

Tonight?

Sure. 7 pm at that gelato place?

Sounds good.

I turn off my phone and spend the rest of the day on the computer, reading about being transgender. There's a lot of stuff about puberty-suppressing drugs, but I'm pretty sure Alex hasn't done that. You need to have your parents' permission, for one thing, and lots of support from your family. And money. Not an option for Alex. One doctor says that *without puberty-suppressing drugs, transgender kids are at risk for depression and suicide, and are subject to bullying, abuse, alienation and harassment.* I hope Alex hasn't ever been depressed or suicidal, but I wouldn't be surprised if he had. I would be if I'd been born into his family. Maybe Meredith saved him from that. In which case I should be grateful to her.

I find an article called "What Happens When You Find the One…And He's Nothing—Nothing—Like You Expected?" I don't actually believe in the concept of "the one," but the author has a lot of interesting things to say about falling in love with a trans guy. She says real love, true love, *shakes you up inside like a Boggle board, jangling all your letters into wholly new words, some you've never seen before but recognize instantly nonetheless.*

She also says that *to be trans is to feel the truth so acutely you can't fake it. It is to be so consumed with the truth of who you are that you are willing to risk everything to inhabit it. To refuse to be what other people have decided you are—this is an act of courage few individuals dare try.*

I wonder if I have the courage to inhabit my own truth. I wonder what that truth is. I do feel jangled. But I also feel excited—and hopeful. Like maybe this can work.

I borrow Mom's car after dinner and get to the gelato place early. I'm staring into the gelato case, trying to decide between mango and bacio, when someone comes up behind me and puts their hands over my eyes.

"My treat," Alex says. "Let me surprise you."

You've already done that, I want to say, but I put my hands over his and we stand there for a few seconds. I can smell him—nothing gross, just a hint of something minty, like toothpaste or mouthwash. He also smells vaguely like a cedar tree. His hands are soft and the tiniest bit sweaty. We let our hands drop, and I step back and turn to face him.

"I don't normally like surprises, but I'll make an exception," I say. "Seeing as how I like all their flavors. It's all about the combinations. The explosion in your mouth. The taste on your tongue."

He smiles. I smile back. A woman behind us mutters, "Get a room."

Alex turns to her and says, "We're saving ourselves for marriage."

"After we have some gelato, we're going shopping for purity rings," I add.

The woman pulls her phone out of her purse and starts playing Candy Crush.

Alex grins at me and says, "Can you find a table for us, sweetheart?"

"Certainly, my darling," I reply. I lean over and whisper to the woman, "Isn't he adorable?"

She scowls and pokes her screen.

I find a table and watch Alex at the counter. He samples quite a few flavors, licking the tiny spoons one by one, a look of deep concentration on his face. The girl behind the counter doesn't seem to mind. In fact, judging by her body language—the hair flips, the way she smiles at him every time she hands him another spoon—I think she's flirting with him. It's a relief to see I'm not the only one who thinks he's hot.

He's wearing his usual outfit—shorts and a buttoned shirt—but today's shirt is one I haven't seen before. It's got very fine red-and-white stripes—from a distance it looks pink. His shorts are navy-blue plaid. Both the shirt and the shorts look as if they have been ironed. His hair is starting to curl around his ears. Nothing about him looks feminine to me. His features are strong: straight nose, broad forehead, high cheekbones. His mouth is wide, his lips full but not pouty. He has a few freckles on his cheeks and some on his forearms. He's not nearly as pretty as Johnny Depp or Zac Efron. His hands and feet are big. His chest is flat. I wonder if he's wearing a binder.

When he comes back to the table, he is carrying a round tray loaded with six little white bowls of gelato, two spoons and two glasses of ice water. He places the tray on the table and then whips a red bandanna out of his pocket.

"What's that for?" I ask.

He comes around behind me and blindfolds me with the bandanna.

"A challenge. For every flavor you guess correctly, you can ask me a question. For every one you get wrong,

I get to ask you a question. We have to answer honestly and quickly—we don't want the gelato to melt. Fair?"

If I was being my usual sensible self, I'd probably say, *Why don't we just ask each other questions without all this fuss?* But level-headed Harry is nowhere in sight tonight. Slightly giddy Harriet has taken her place. Nevertheless, I'm glad I can't see if people are staring at us. And I know my gelato, so with any luck I'll learn something about Alex. "Bring it on."

"Ready?" he says.

I nod and open my mouth. A spoonful of gelato lands on my tongue. "This one's too easy," I say. "Honey lavender."

"Correct," Alex says. "Your question?"

I consider leading with the big question—when did you know you weren't a girl?—but I settle for "What are your parents like?"

"My parents?" He sounds surprised. I wish I could see his face. "My parents are"—he pauses—"ignorant."

"Ignorant? That's it?"

"Yup. Next flavor."

The next spoonful is a flavor I've never had before. I take a wild guess—guava sorbet—but I'm wrong; it's passion fruit.

"What do you want to know?" I ask him.

He's silent for a moment, and then he says, "Have you ever been in love?"

So much for holstering the big guns.

"Yes," I say. "I think so. Maybe. I don't know."

"Not very conclusive," Alex says. Is it my imagination, or does he sound relieved? "Next flavor."

I guess the next one correctly—it's watermelon, which is tricky because it's so subtle—and ask Alex if he ever disagrees with Meredith.

"Not very often," he answers.

After I identify dulce de leche, I ask why.

"Because she's my best friend and she's on my side. We're a team. Have been since we were six."

When I draw a blank on zabaione, he asks me if I'll reconsider meeting my donor.

At which point I pull off the bandanna and toss it on the table. It lands in the passion fruit sorbet. My eyes are stinging, and I don't think it's just from being blindfolded.

"So is that what this is really all about?"

He shakes his head. "She told me he contacted her. I just wondered if you were curious. That's all. She and Lucy are pretty excited."

"Yeah, I know. I've got, like, twenty texts from them."

"So?"

I shrug and say, "Still not interested." Even though I might be.

Alex points at the only gelato we haven't tasted. "One for the road?" he asks, scooping a bit onto a spoon and holding it out for me. I lean forward and eat it. So easy.

"Stracciatella."

"Correctomundo. And your final question?"

I take a deep breath and say, "When were you going to tell me you were born a girl?"

Alex drops the spoon in a puddle of dulce de leche and stands up. "Let's get out of here," he says.

I look at the rapidly melting gelato and grab another bite of honey lavender. Then I pick up the sticky red bandanna and follow Alex out of the restaurant. He's moving fast down 3rd Avenue, past Benaroya Hall. I'm almost running to keep up with him. I can't tell if he's upset or angry or what.

We cross University, then Seneca, and then he turns left on Spring and heads for the library. Not exactly what I'd call private, but I don't argue when he sits down on a bench under some trees near the library's entrance.

"I love this place," he says. "I couldn't believe it when I first saw it. Such an amazing building, and it's full of books. Paradise. It's between work and home, so I come here a lot. Always calms me down."

"Where do you live?" I ask. I sit down beside him on the bench, but not too close.

"Beacon Hill. With Meredith. It's tiny—I sleep on a pullout couch—but it's all we can afford right now. I want to move. Maybe to Georgetown or Columbia City."

"Columbia City? Really?" Columbia City isn't exactly most people's first pick in Seattle.

He shrugs. "I like it. It's…I don't know…authentic. Meredith wants to move to the U District. Maybe we'll end up there."

"Ooh. Frat boys and Huskies' games," I say. "Is that Meredith's scene?"

"Not really. It's sure not mine. But we can't afford Capitol Hill or Queen Anne."

"How about Edmonds?" I nudge him with my elbow.

He smiles. "Now that's too far. No one will ever give me a ride out there."

We sit in silence for a few minutes, watching people go in and out of the library.

"How did you know?" he finally asks.

I'm about to make up some bullshit story, but then I remember another of Verna's sayings: *Begin as you mean to go on, go on as you began.* Lying to Alex wasn't an option. Not if I wanted to have him in my life.

"I called Meredith's parents," I say. "And your mom."

"You what?" For a second, his voice sounds as high as mine.

"I found them online, and I called them."

"Why?"

"Because I wanted to know more about Meredith. I know it sounds dumb, but I couldn't figure out how she could have done all those things—dancing in Denver, volunteering at a shelter in Boise and working on an organic farm. It just didn't make sense. So I did some research. Missoula newspapers, Google, Facebook. It wasn't hard."

"And did they tell you about me?" It sounds as if he's gritting his teeth, each word struggling to escape.

I don't want him to think that Barbara and Mark have betrayed him, so I shake my head and say, "No. I found a picture of your Little League team. Danielle and Meredith. I thought you had a twin sister. Meredith's parents told me you didn't, that's all."

Alex turns away from me. The back of his neck is splotchy, and his shoulders are hunched.

"And then I called your mom, and she told me that Alex and Danielle are the same person." No way was I going to tell him how harsh his mom had been.

"Did she tell you about the time I ended up in hospital after my dad beat me with my own baseball bat? And about that scar on my leg? That's from when my brother and his friends jumped me. My brother had a knife." Alex's voice is muffled. I have to lean in to hear him. "Did she tell you that she took me to this crazy Pentecostal exorcist when I was twelve? And my brother told everyone at school I was gay? Which I'm not, by the way. Did she tell you that other kids called me *he-she* or *it*? Did she tell you that a bunch of guys shoved my head in the toilet bowl when I tried to use the boys' washroom at school?"

"No, she didn't tell me any of that stuff. We didn't talk for long." I want to put my arms around him, tell him that I understand, but it would sound false. It would be false. I don't really understand. I've transcribed dozens of horror stories for Mom, but I don't know the girls. Except for Annabeth, their lives don't intersect with mine. This is real. This is someone I care about. I can't pretend to know what it's like to have your own family hate you. No wonder Meredith is so important to him.

"You didn't give them our numbers or anything, did you?" he says.

"They didn't ask. And I wouldn't have even if they had."

"Meredith isn't ready to talk to her parents. Maybe after she meets her donor…"

I don't want to talk about the donor thing. I don't even really want to talk about the trans thing. Alex turns to look at me, and I can see the question on his face: *Are we okay?*

In answer, I reach out and take his hand in mine. We sit side by side, watching a tiny girl stagger out of the library with a huge pile of books.

"I was going to tell you," he finally says, "but I was afraid, you know? A lot of girls would freak out."

"You thought I would freak out? Me? The most level-headed girl on the planet?"

He laughs. "Yeah, even you. It's kind of a big deal."

"Yeah, I get that. And I did freak out a bit. It was a shock."

He grips my hand a bit tighter. "I'm not sure what to tell you."

"Anything you want," I say. "I'm not going to freak out again, I promise."

"I started hormone therapy when we came here," he says. "Things are starting to change—my voice is lower,

I've got serious stubble. I wear a light binder, but I'm saving up for top surgery."

"So you've traded a bra for a binder," I say. "And you're shaving your face instead shaving your legs and pits."

Alex smiles weakly. "That's one way of looking at it, I guess."

"I'm sorry," I say. "I'm just trying to, you know, lighten the mood."

"I get it," Alex says. "You don't need to apologize. But you're the first girl I've really wanted to tell. The first girl I've really liked. So I'm glad you know. I'm a man—whatever that means. That's part of why I came to Seattle—to live as a man, openly, in a place where no one knows me as *that freak*. It doesn't mean I tell everybody I'm trans though."

My hand is getting sweaty holding his, but I don't pull away. Instead, I lean in and kiss him on the cheek. I can feel some fuzziness under my lips. And I can taste a bit of salt.

"Do you like fish tacos?" I ask, pulling him to his feet.

"Yes, why?" he says.

"I know a place," I reply.

"Thanks," he says.

"For what? Knowing a good taco place?"

"For not freaking out. Or running away."

"What? And miss seeing Churchill again?"

When I get home, Mom has gone to bed, but the light is still on in her room. She's sitting up in bed, reading.

"Fun night?" she asks.

I slip off my shoes and lie down on the bed next to her. She puts her book on the night table and takes off her reading glasses. Her pillows smell of orange blossoms, and I think of Alex and me in Nori's garden.

"I need to tell you something," I say.

"Okay." She snuggles down next to me, our heads almost touching.

"You know I really like Alex, right?"

She nods.

I wonder for a moment if I'm about to betray Alex's confidence, but I have to talk to someone. And Mom is like a vault. I trust her.

"He was born a girl."

"Yes," Mom says. "I suspected as much."

I prop myself up on one elbow and stare down at her. "You did?"

"I've worked with some trans kids," Mom says. "Maybe I'm just more aware of what transitioning can look like. And maybe it's a good thing you didn't notice. That you simply responded to him as a person."

"So you don't think it's weird?"

She shoots me a stern look. "Weird? No. Difficult? Yes."

"But he doesn't have a—you know—a penis."

"So? If it walks like a boy and talks like a boy…"

"Then it is a boy. I know, but it's not that simple." I sigh and flop back onto the pillow. "And to top it all off, our donor contacted Meredith."

Now Mom sits up. "That's big news."

I bury my face in the pillow and groan. "Why does everything have to happen at once?"

She laughs and rubs my back. "I've wondered that myself many times. Unfortunately, we don't get to pick and choose what life throws at us. Right now, the best thing you can do is get some sleep." She pulls the duvet over me and then turns out the light. Her voice floats over me in the darkness. "Things will look better in the morning, Harry. I promise."

ELEVEN

WHEN I TURN my phone on the next morning, there are two more texts, three missed calls and a voice mail. I listen to the voice mail first. It's from Byron.

Hey, Harry, he says. *I know we said we wouldn't talk, but it's hard. New York City is cool, but I miss the coast—a lot. And I miss you. I've met a few people here, but not anyone I want to hang out with. Zach's mom and dad say I can stay with them if I decide to come back to Seattle. Can you call me? I get that you might not want to. Hope you do though. See ya.*

Shit. He sounds so confused. That makes two of us. Part of me wants to call and tell him to come home. Tell him we can pick up where we left off. Another part of me wants to call and tell him the truth—or at least part of the truth: I've met someone else, but I still want to be friends. I want to imagine him roaming around New York with

138

a girl who adores him, wearing horn-rimmed glasses and eating designer donuts at some trendy pop-up restaurant. Most of all, I want him to be happy so I can be happy too. Maybe he feels the same way. Maybe I'll call him and see how it goes.

I sigh and move on to the texts.

One is from Meredith: **Pls call me. It's important.**

The other is from my friend Gwen: **Back from France soon. SOOO many stories.**

Gwen and I have been friends since sixth grade. Her boyfriend, Zach, is Byron's best friend. We spent a lot of time together, the four of us. Gwen thought Byron and I were crazy to break up. She's a true romantic—always has been. *Love conquers all. Absence makes the heart grow fonder. Love makes the world go round. Love means never having to say you're sorry.* To give her credit, she's also super smart and very funny. She wants to be a pediatric oncologist, for god's sake. She'd probably think dating a trans guy was cool, but I don't think I can talk about it with her yet, especially on Skype. I might tell her about the donor thing though. She's a good listener.

I decide to call Lucy, who shrieks when she hears my voice.

"Where have you been? I've been so worried. Didn't you get my texts? Are you okay?"

When she finally winds down, I say, "I'm fine. Just busy. I turned off my phone. But I heard the news. Meredith must be stoked."

"She was right, Harry. He's from here. Not right here, but close by. Whidbey Island. Right now he's in Mexico, so we're going to email first. Maybe talk on the phone. Get to know each other a bit before we meet."

"I thought you didn't want to meet him."

"I didn't think I did, but now I'm curious. I've talked to Angela and Nori about it, and they say it's up to me. But they'll want to be there too. Can you imagine? Angela will be all kind and caring, and Nori will grill him about his life choices." She laughs, and I can't help it—I laugh too.

"I really want you to be part of this, Harry," she continues. "You know, like the three musketeers. One for all and all for one."

"Then my mom would want to get involved. And Verna."

"And Alex," Lucy says. "Don't forget Alex."

As if I could.

"Poor guy," I say.

"Alex? Why?"

"Not Alex. Our donor. He won't know what hit him. Three daughters, three moms, a granny and a best friend. Probably more than he bargained for. He may regret coming out of hiding."

"Do you think so?" Lucy sounds worried, as if it hasn't occurred to her that it might have been a tough decision for him. "Meredith says he seems really nice. I'm a bit scared to email him. What if he doesn't like me?"

I laugh again. "Not like you? He'd have to be crazy."

"Will you help me?" she asks.

"With what?"

"With my email."

"Um, sure. I guess. If you want me to."

"Can you come over now?"

"Can I have some breakfast first?"

"I'll make you breakfast. Bacon, eggs, toast, whatever you like."

"Sounds good. I'll see if I can get Mom to drive me."

"Pancakes?"

"Stop," I say. "You had me at bacon."

Mom has some errands to run, so she agrees to drive me to Lucy's. When we get there, before I get out of the car, she says, "It's okay if you want to meet him, you know. In case you were worried about how I'd feel."

Lucy runs down the front steps before I can reply and knocks on Mom's window. When Mom rolls it down, Lucy says, "Angela's home for a couple of hours. She wants you to come in for breakfast. We've got muffins in the oven if you don't want eggs. Banana-chocolate chip. They're awesome."

Mom smiles and turns to me. "Okay with you if I stay? I know you and Lucy have things to discuss."

"Can't pass up your favorite muffins," I say, and she turns off the car.

Lucy bounces along beside us as we go up the path to the house. "I can't believe I'm so excited about meeting our donor. I mean, I've barely given him a second thought before. It's weird. Angela and Nori want us to take it slowly, but that's not my style, you know?"

"I know," I say. "But I'm with your moms on this one. Slow and steady wins the race, as Verna would say."

"If you're a turtle," Lucy says. "But Meredith is acting like she's got cold feet too. And she was the one who was all gung ho to begin with."

"Reality will do that to you," Mom says.

When we go into the house, we're hit with the best smell in the world (next to Mom's cologne)—bacon and fresh baking. Angela comes out of the kitchen and hugs Mom and me.

"I'm so glad you're here, Della. I bake when I get antsy. And then I eat it all."

"Glad to help," Mom says. "And glad to hear you're antsy too. I thought maybe I was the only one."

"I know," Angela says. "We knew this day might come, but it feels different than I thought it would. More… fraught. Hence the baking. Nori doesn't seem concerned at all. So it's nice to have someone to talk to."

We sit down at the harvest table in the kitchen. Nobody talks much. We're too busy stuffing our faces. Lucy, despite her size, eats more than anyone else. Four slices of bacon, a mountain of eggs, three slices of toast with peanut butter and jam, two muffins. She washes it down with mugs of milky coffee. When she notices me watching her, she grins and says, "Yeah, I know. Nori says I eat like a stevedore, whatever that means. I've always been that way. Right, Angela?"

"From the day she was born," Angela says. "I thought Adam would be the one emptying the refrigerator, but he eats like a sparrow compared to Lucy."

"She's like a hummingbird," I say. "Eating her body weight every day. You should have called her Anna."

"Why Anna?" Lucy asks.

"They're the only type of hummingbird that over-winters here," I tell her. When Lucy gapes at me, I add, "School project, seventh grade."

"Cool," she says as we clear the table, leaving Mom and Angela to their tea.

Lucy's room has turquoise walls and an orange paisley duvet with matching throw pillows. There are clothes everywhere—and I mean everywhere. On the floor, on the bed, under the bed, on the turquoise-and-orange-striped armchair by the window, on the bedside table, overflowing the drawers of a huge dresser, spilling out of the closet.

"Wow!" I say. "You have a lot of clothes."

"I know, I know. It drives Nori and Angela crazy. But I buy them myself and I do my own laundry, so they can't say much about it."

I can't imagine functioning in such a mess, but she's obviously used to it.

She sweeps some clothes off a desk and chair, revealing a MacBook Air. I clear the armchair and pull it over next to the desk.

"So here's what I've got." She opens the laptop and turns the screen toward me.

Dear Dr. Ramos, it says.

"That's it?"

She nods. "That's why I need your help. You're good with words, right? I don't want to sound like an idiot."

"Okay. What do you want to say?"

"That's just it. I'm not sure."

I tell her what Mom has always told me when I'm writing something: Be direct. Be yourself. Be brief.

"So tell me what you want to say, and I'll write things down. Then we can edit it into a really good email."

Lucy trades places with me and starts to talk. Fast. I keep telling her to slow down—I'm a good typist, but I'm not that good—and she tries, but she has a *lot* to say. Most of which doesn't make it into the final email.

After two hours, more coffee (for her) and some water for me, this is what we come up with.

Dear Dr. Ramos,
My name is Lucy Tanaka and I am your daughter. I am fifteen years old and I live in Seattle with my two moms, Angela and Nori. I have a half-brother named Adam who is your son with Angela. He's in Portland, Oregon, at school. Another half-brother, Ben, lives in Australia.

I have a great life—I'm very happy. I never thought about contacting you until I met my half-sisters Meredith and Harriet (Harry). Meredith came here from Montana to find you (but you probably already know that). Harriet and I have lived here all our lives. It's weird to think that we might have passed you on the street.

I am a ballet dancer. My moms put me in dance when I was really little because I have a LOT of energy. I love dancing. I teach Baby Ballet on Saturdays. If it was up to me, I would arrange to meet you tomorrow—I hate waiting—but everyone says we should take it slow, get to know each other via email, so that's what I'm doing.

I really appreciate that you got in touch with Meredith. I'm curious how you found out she was looking for you. And I'm really excited to meet you. If that's what you want too. Please email me back a bit about yourself (if you feel like it).

Your daughter,

Lucy

She wants to add her phone number, but I tell her I don't think it's a good idea yet. One thing at a time. She groans and throws a paisley pillow at me. "Why do you always have to be so sensible, Harriet?"

I shrug. "I came out of the womb that way, I guess, just like you came out chugging your weight in breast milk and whirling like a dervish."

"Gross," she says. "Shall we send it?"

"Up to you." I hand her the laptop and she rereads the email. When she hits *Send* and the email whooshes away, I wish I'd added a few lines of my own.

Harriet here. I was against trying to find you, but now I'm not so sure. I look a lot like you. I know you're a donor, not a dad, but now that you've been found, I think I want to meet you. I just don't have the guts to say so.

TWELVE

MOM IS LONG GONE by the time we finish the email, so Angela drops me off at home on her way to work. She doesn't ask about the donor stuff, and I don't volunteer anything. There's a note from Mom on the kitchen table: *Had to go to the college. I left you a transcription I need done right away. Hope you had fun with Lucy. I ate too many muffins. Will be hitting the gym later. Grilled chicken for dinner?*

I gather up all the stuff I need for transcribing—laptop, earbuds, tape recorder—and sit at the kitchen table. The girl's name is Brandi. She goes to high school, even though she has no home. She wants to study law and be an advocate for poor people. A while ago her dad lost his job—he was some kind of executive—and started drinking a lot. Her stay-at-home mom had no income. One of her little brothers (she has three) has epilepsy.

The family lost their home and dear old dad disappeared into the bottle, leaving mom in a shelter with four kids. They were on a wait list for subsidized housing, but nothing was big enough for four kids. Apparently there are rules about how many kids you can stuff into one bedroom, especially if one kid has special needs.

When Brandi turned seventeen, she decided to take care of herself while her mom got back on her feet. She couch-surfs and eats out of Dumpsters or gets bread and peanut butter from the food bank, dragging herself to school every day. The school has no idea she's homeless. She stays at the school, doing homework in the library, until the janitors kick her out. Sometimes she hides out in the girls' change room after the school closes. Then she has a shower, washes her underwear and sleeps on a yoga mat she found in the Lost and Found. She doesn't do drugs or drink. She never turns tricks. She makes a bit of money panhandling and allows herself one Subway meal a week. Her grades are good, but she's worried they won't be good enough to earn her a scholarship for university. She looks after her little brothers on Sundays to give her mom a break.

The girl is a freakin' saint. Her best friend from high school sneaks Brandi into her room at night and brings her food when she can, but Brandi won't let her tell her parents that Brandi has no home to go to. She's afraid of Social Services. Going into foster care seems worse to her than never knowing where you're going to sleep.

Once her mom gets housing, she'll probably go there for meals and a shower, but only if it doesn't jeopardize her family's stability.

I stop typing and take out my earbuds. Every time I do a transcription, I'm reminded of how good my life is. Roof over head—check. Regular meals—check. Good school—check. Nice clothes—check. Access to a car—check. Friends—check. Family—check. Money for university—check. Maybe that's why Mom hired me: to give me some perspective. If so, it's working. I like my sheltered life, but maybe it's time to shake it up a bit.

I take a deep breath, open a new email message and start typing.

Dear Dr. Ramos,

My name is Harriet Jacobs, known as Harry. I don't know how much Meredith has told you about me, but I thought I would write and say hello. I live with my mom here in Seattle. Everyone on DSR recommends that you take it slow when you first connect with your donor (and vice versa), and that's fine with me. Actually, I told Meredith and Lucy I didn't want to meet you, but that turns out not to be true. I'm not exactly sure why. Just to be clear, I don't need or want you to be my dad. But I do want to know some things, so I hope you don't mind answering a few questions.

1. Where did you grow up?
2. What kind of doctor are you?

3. Do you have any children (other than donor kids)?

4. Are you married?

5. When were you a donor?

6. How did you find out about us?

7. Do you want to meet us?

8. Are your parents still alive?

9. Do you have any siblings? If so, do they have kids?

10. What is your favorite food?

I'm sure I'll think of other things, but that's it for now.

Sincerely,

Harry

I send the email before I can think better of it.

Now all I have to do is wait. I'm about to Skype Gwen when the doorbell rings. When I open the door, I immediately regret not changing into something nicer than the yoga pants and gray hoodie I wore to Lucy's.

Alex is standing on my doorstep, holding a florist's box, the kind long-stemmed red roses come in. I like roses in gardens, but I hate the kind that are grown in South America and get shipped here in refrigerated containers. They don't even smell like roses. *Frankenroses*, Mom calls them. *The ultimate clichéd romantic gesture.* I wouldn't have pegged Alex as that guy, and it's not Valentine's Day, but I fear the worst.

"Hey," I say. "This is a surprise. How did you find out where I live?" It's not the friendliest greeting, but he's caught me off guard.

"I have my ways," he says. I must look skeptical, because he adds, "Okay. I called Verna. I wanted to surprise you."

"Mission accomplished," I say, trying to remember if I've brushed my hair recently.

He shifts from foot to foot on the porch, and I step back to let him inside. Compared to Lucy's house, ours is nothing special, but it's nothing to be ashamed of either. I lead him into the kitchen, where my laptop is still open on the table. He puts the long white box on the table and leans against the counter.

"Want to see what I wrote to my donor?" I say.

"You wrote to him? I thought you didn't want anything to do with him."

"I changed my mind. I'm allowed to do that, you know."

He nods and says, "I'm sure it was a very rational decision." He's smiling when he says it, so I know he's teasing me.

I punch him lightly on the shoulder and pull out a chair for him. We sit side by side as he reads my email. When he's done, he tilts his chair onto its two back legs and says, "Very thorough. Excellent tone. Not too needy. Friendly but not excessively so. Respectful."

"I try," I say. "It's weird though. I've gone from not wanting to contact him at all to wishing he'd set up a meeting. And I don't really know why."

"Does there always have to be a why?" he asks, still teetering on the chair. It's making me anxious, watching him balance. "Maybe he's communicating with you on, I don't know, a cellular level."

I snort. "Yeah right."

"Not everything is logical, Harry," he says softly. He lets the front legs of his chair bump down and pushes the box across the table toward me.

Please, please don't be red roses, I think as I lift the lid off the box. No roses, thank god. A lot of crumpled white tissue paper fills the box, and after I push it aside, I reach in and pull out a wooden rectangle maybe a foot and a half long, a couple of inches high and an inch wide, tapered at both ends. I have no idea what it is. The faded label reads *Globemaster*. There are two brass-trimmed holes—one in the top and one on the side. The one on the side looks like a porthole. I examine it more closely and see tiny tubes filled with yellow liquid in the holes. Bubbles in the liquid move around as I turn the thing over in my hands.

Alex takes it away from me and places it on the table in front of me. "It's called a spirit level. Carpenters use them, although now they have digital ones. I saw this one at a thrift shop near my house and thought of you. A level for the level-headed." He points to one of the little vials. The bubble is sitting slightly to the left of one of two lines painted on the vial. "See? Your table isn't level."

I laugh and get up and put the level on the counter. It's also a bit off. I wander around the house, Alex trailing behind me, trying to find something that is actually level.

The dining-room table is close, the living-room floor is way off, and most of the stuff hanging on our walls is wonky. Alex and I straighten the pictures as we go.

"I like your house," he says. "It feels lived-in."

"You mean it's messy," I say. There are books and mugs strewn around the house, but the carpets are relatively clean, the dirty dishes are in the dishwasher, and the garbage isn't overflowing the bin.

"No," he says. "That's not what I mean."

"I know," I say. I pick the level up and balance it on my head. "So—am I really that level-headed?"

I walk across the living room toward him, like a debutante at a deportment class. When I get close enough for him to see the bubble in the level, he leans in and looks into my eyes instead. "Not as level-headed as you think," he whispers. I stand very still, my arms at my sides, as he kisses me. His lips are soft and the kiss is gentle, almost tentative. I want it to last forever. I can feel the level slipping, slipping, slipping as I lean into the kiss. He catches it as it falls and slides it onto the couch, his lips never breaking contact with mine. I close my eyes as the kiss continues. Our bodies are only meeting at our lips, but I am hyperaware of his body. The breadth of his shoulders, the long slope of his back, the curve of his ass, the length of his legs. I feel weightless, as if the kiss has created an atmosphere in which I am free to float and experience all the sensations of this one thing. My lips feel warm and swollen; my breathing is becoming ragged. I stagger slightly and Alex pulls me toward him until my head rests on his shoulder, and we sway together, like marathon dancers holding each other up when everyone else has collapsed.

And then Alex's phone rings. The ringtone is "You've Got a Friend in Me," from *Toy Story*. I don't need a crystal ball to know who it is.

"Shit, shit, shit," Alex says as he pulls the phone out of his pocket. "I gotta take this. I'm sorry." He walks away from me, his shoulders hunched, and I hear him say, "Hey, Merry. What's up? You okay?" before he opens the front door and steps out onto the porch.

I sit on the couch and fume, turning the spirit level over in my hands, watching it transform from the most romantic gesture ever into an old block of wood with holes in it. I put it on the coffee table and glare at it. Apparently the coffee table is exactly level. I can't believe he took her call. It seems as if the biggest impediment to our relationship isn't the fact that he was born female; it's that he's a wimp when it comes to Meredith. Did she know he was coming to see me today? Did she call on purpose, to interrupt us, ruin our moment? I wouldn't put it past her.

The front door opens and Alex comes back in and sits beside me on the couch. "I have to go," he says. "I need to see Meredith before I go in to work. She's freaking out about Dr. Ramos. She thinks he's going to reject her or something. Like Mark did."

"Mark rejected her?"

"Well, that's how it felt to her, I guess. He just withdrew when she was in high school. Didn't give her the support she needed. She completely derailed. Drugs, alcohol, a couple of pregnancies. A lot of fights. It was really hard to watch. I was the only person she trusted, the one she called when she was in trouble."

"And now she thinks she's going to get the kind of support she wants from a complete stranger? That's crazy." The minute the words are out of my mouth, I regret them.

"Is it? Maybe he can give her what she needs." Alex's voice is as level as the coffee table.

What she needs is a swift kick in the ass, I think, but what do I know? Maybe Mark and Barbara did let her down when she was out of control, but I kind of doubt it.

Alex stands up and looks down at me. "I fucked it up again, didn't I?" he says.

"Kind of," I say.

"I don't know what to do," he says. "She gets so down on herself…"

"And you're the fixer. I get it. So go fix her." I stand up and cross my arms over my chest. "Thanks for the level. I'm sure it will come in handy if I ever decide to become a carpenter."

He reaches out and touches my cheek. I move away, but not before the hairs on my arm stand up.

"I'll fix this, I promise," he says. "She just needs to understand that I won't abandon her too."

I roll my eyes. "Good luck with that," I say as I open the door for him.

Turns out fury makes me dry-eyed, not teary. I'm furious at Alex, furious at Meredith, furious at myself. How could I have been so stupid? Thinking it would all work out with a trans boy who's attached at the hip to my needy half-sister. Who am I kidding? The odds were against us from the get-go. The only person I'm not furious at is Lucy, but there's no way I'm telling her any of this. For some reason she thinks Meredith walks on water. The best I can do is try to protect her.

When Mom gets home, I'm in the middle of making fajitas for dinner. The laundry is done and folded, and there are brownies (no bacon) in the oven.

"Brownies?" Mom laughs. "Guess I'll be back at the gym tomorrow. How was your day?"

"Good," I say. "I did that transcription for you; did some laundry too."

"Sounds like a productive day," she says. "What's that?" She points at the spirit level, which is sitting on top of the fridge, which is apparently not level either.

"It's a spirit level. Alex gave it to me."

"It's quite lovely," she says.

"I guess," I say. "Do you want onions on your fajitas?"

"No onions. So Alex came by today?"

"Just to drop off the level on his way to work."

"Very sweet," she says. "But you don't look that happy."

"It's complicated," I say.

"Isn't it always?" she says.

"Is that why you never married?" I ask. "Or had a long-term relationship? And don't give me all that bullshit about how busy you were raising me and going to school. Lots of people do those things and have relationships too."

"That's true," she says. "Can I pour myself a drink before we get into this? I think this calls for more than a glass of red wine." She pulls a bottle of tonic water out of the fridge and a bottle of gin out of the cupboard and makes herself a tall drink. Then she sits at the kitchen table and takes a long sip. "My parents had a terrible marriage. I've told you that."

"That's about all you've told me."

"I didn't think you needed the details, since you were never going to meet them. But maybe I was wrong."

"Yeah, you were," I say. "So tell me."

Mom sighs, takes a gulp of her drink and says, "They had one of those 'stay together for the sake of the kids' relationships. Perfect on the outside, vicious on the inside, like an eclair filled with shit. Apparently they were very happy until they had kids, and then it all went to hell. My mom loved me and my brother, Robbie, more than anything. More than Dad. At least, that's what he said when he got hammered. Robbie started drinking when he was thirteen. He died in a car accident—he was driving drunk—when he was sixteen. After that, my parents ignored me and concentrated on drinking and making each other miserable. I ran away and came out here. Then I met Verna, and you know the rest of the story. I had you. That was all I trusted myself with—you and Verna and my work. I was afraid that if I added in a relationship, I would become like my parents."

By the time she stops speaking, we are both pretty choked up. I think about all that she has denied herself—a lot of it for my sake—and it makes me sad.

"Was there ever anyone…?"

"Yes," she says. "There was. Not too long ago. Remember Ray, the boatbuilder? The one I went out with last year? He had one of those things." She points to the spirit level. "We started to get pretty serious. I broke up with him, even though I really cared for him."

I remember Ray. I liked him. He played the banjo in a bluegrass band with his brother and his cousin. "Oh, Mom," I say. "You're never going to be like your mom and dad. Never. It's just not possible."

"I can't take the chance." She takes a swig of her drink. "Nature versus nurture, right? No one really knows how it works. That's why I studied sociology. To try and figure it out."

"And?"

She laughs. "And I still don't know. Probably never will. And here I sit, drinking my mom's favorite drink, telling my lovely daughter horror stories."

"You don't need to do that anymore," I say.

"Do what? Drink?"

"Give up things for me. I don't want you to. I'm not a little kid anymore. You're not going to turn into a monster and hurt me. For one thing, Verna wouldn't allow it. Can you imagine?"

Mom shrugs. "Maybe you're right."

"I am."

"I'll make you a deal," she says.

"Okay."

"I won't shy away from whatever life throws at me if you won't."

"What does that mean?"

"I think you know." She points at the spirit level. "You're too young not to take a chance, and I'm too old."

"You think?"

"I do."

I reach across the table and take her hand and shake it.

"Deal," I say.

"Deal," she replies.

THIRTEEN

LUCY CALLS ME the morning after my heart-to-heart with Mom. I've already taken the dogs for a walk and am getting ready to go to the salon. I need to keep busy.

"Meredith's freaking out," she says. "I mean *freaking out.*"

"About what?" I ask.

"About Dr. Ramos. Apparently he hasn't responded to her latest email, and she's convinced he hates her."

I roll my eyes. "Have you heard from him?"

"Nope," she says cheerfully. "But then, I'm not looking for a daddy. Meredith is. She says her dad—the one who raised her—abandoned her when she needed him most, and she thinks her bio-dad is doing the same."

"Isn't it a bit soon to assume that?" I want to tell her about calling Mark and Barbara, but I'm afraid she'll go straight to Meredith and all hell will break loose. Instead I say, "I wrote to him too. Last night."

"You did?" she says. "That's awesome. Now we can all go together to meet him when he gets back from Mexico."

"Assuming he wants to meet us," I reply. "He might not. Three teenage daughters coming out of nowhere? How terrifying is that!"

Lucy laughs. "We're not that bad, are we?"

Not you and me, I want to say. But Meredith? She's another story.

"I gotta run to class," Lucy says before I can answer. "Text me if you hear anything, okay?"

When I get there, the salon is hopping, and I stay for the whole day, answering the phone, shampooing clients, sweeping up hair, making coffee, taking care of some toddlers while their moms get their hair cut, running to the bank for change, getting sandwiches at the deli across the street. Verna drives me home at the end of the day and comes in to have tea with Mom, who is on the phone in her office.

"I'm going to jump in the shower," I tell Verna.

There are dishes in the sink, and she starts to rinse them and put them in the dishwasher. "I'll do that," I say. "Mom will flip if she finds you doing my chores."

She waves me off and fills the kettle. "I can handle Della," she says. "You run along."

In my room, I check my phone for messages. Nothing. I turn on my computer to check my email. Nothing. I have to admit it—I'm disappointed and a bit upset. I can't seem to differentiate the strands of confusion and hurt. It's one giant ugly mass of emotional junk, like that island of garbage that floats in the Pacific Ocean.

Over the next three days, I don't hear from anyone but Lucy. She doesn't seem concerned that our donor has gone AWOL, but I'm starting to get seriously pissed off.

Finally, on Friday evening, an email arrives from Dr. Ramos while I am watching a movie on my laptop.

Dear Lucy, Meredith and Harriet,
Thank you for your emails. It has been quite overwhelming to connect with you. I hope you can forgive me for taking so long to reply. I needed to think about what I was going to say. And I hope you don't mind that I am emailing you as a group.

You have many questions, some of which I will happily answer here, some of which might be better answered in person. Obviously, there is no rulebook for this situation; the best I can do is proceed with caution and respect. As my siblings would tell you, I am not the most gregarious person in the world, so please do not read anything into my reticence.

I am 61 years old and I have been an ER physician for many years. I retired last year after my wife, Alissa, died of breast cancer. I live on Whidbey Island, where I read, dig in my garden and listen to music. I am quite a good cook and a very bad guitarist. Not very exciting, but there it is. I got enough excitement working in the ER to last three lifetimes.

I donated sperm often when I was a medical student. As you may know, sperm can be frozen for a very long time and still remain viable. Alissa and I never had children—she was unable to conceive. And yes, I do see the irony of that. The very sad irony. I have three brothers (one is my identical twin) and two sisters, all in or near Seattle, and too many nieces and nephews to count (not really—I have three nieces and six nephews ranging in age from 4 to 30). I see them as often as I can but not as often as I'd like.

I heard about your Facebook page, Meredith, through one of my nephews. He showed it to his father, my twin brother Bernard. There was some confusion at first, since my nephew thought it was a picture of his father. After reassuring his son, Bernard showed it to the rest of my siblings. Pretty soon I had the whole family after me to contact you, including my mother, who is 90 now, but still very much a force of nature. My father died many years ago. Everyone wanted me to contact "my" children, although I kept telling them I had no claim to call you mine except biologically.

So here we are. I hope I have answered enough of your questions. I would like very much to meet you, but it will have to wait. I am helping set up a clinic in my father's home town in Mexico. I will probably be here at least three more months. In the meantime, I am happy to continue to exchange emails with you all. I hope this is not too disappointing.

Yours truly,

Daniel Ramos

PS. Harriet, my favorite food varies with the season, but I always love a good piece of pie.

PPS. My Internet connection is intermittent. Please don't be alarmed if you don't hear back from me right away.

My first thought is, Well, he must be okay if he likes pie! Strange what the mind latches on to. But I do love pie. Then my phone rings, and Lucy is squealing and shrieking and saying "Omigod" over and over. When she calms down a bit, she tells me that she and Meredith were together when they read the email. They're at a coffee shop now, celebrating with carrot cake. No mention of Alex.

"Meredith must be thrilled," I say, imagining her sitting next to Lucy, listening to our conversation.

"She's on the phone with Alex. She can't stop crying. I think she's kind of bummed that he's still in Mexico. Aren't you excited?"

"Sure," I say. "He sounds really nice."

Lucy laughs. "He sounds like you. Calm, rational. Not like that's a bad thing. Somebody has to be calm. Right, Meredith? Meredith says hi, by the way. Wait, I'm gonna put you on speaker. She's off the phone now."

"Hi, Meredith," I say. "Great news, hey?"

Meredith sniffles and says, "It's wonderful." She sounds as if she has a terrible cold.

"Too bad we can't meet him right away," I say. "But maybe it's better this way. Gives us a chance to get to know him a bit first."

Meredith blows her nose and says, "I suppose," but she doesn't sound convinced.

"We could go over to Whidbey anyway," Lucy says.

"Yeah, we could go and check out his house," I add.

"That's a terrible idea." Meredith sounds as if she's frowning.

"I was just kidding," I say. What is her problem? She seems to have absolutely no sense of humor.

"Maybe we should do a family thing," Lucy suggests. "All the moms, Verna, Alex, the three of us. Take a picnic, go to the beach."

"And Churchill," I add.

"Who's Churchill?" Lucy asks.

"A dog at the shelter where Alex works," Meredith says. "How do you get to the island?"

"The ferry goes from Mukilteo," I say. "Only takes about twenty minutes. We used to rent a cabin on Whidbey when I was little. I love it there. I'll check the schedule and talk to Mom and Verna."

"Road trip," Lucy shrieks. "It's gonna be awesome. The three amigos, right, guys?"

"More like *tres hermanas*. Three sisters," I say.

Lucy cackles. "Call me later, Harriet. I'll talk to my moms. Then I'm gonna call Adam. And Ben. I don't even care what time it is in Australia!"

Once we say our goodbyes, I sit and stare at the phone.

I want to call Alex and talk to him about the email, but he already knows what's happening. If he wants to call me, he can. Maybe Meredith is plotting how to endear herself to Dr. Ramos. I'm sure Alex will support her whatever she does. I hate how bitter that suddenly makes me feel. It's an unpleasant sensation, like biting down on tinfoil when you're eating something delicious.

I check the ferry schedule, shoot both sisters a text about times and go to bed. I read Dr. Ramos's email once more before I turn out the light. Maybe Lucy is right—he does sound like me: level-headed and a bit dull. We should get along just fine.

The next morning when I get up, Mom is sitting at the kitchen table, drinking coffee and reading something on her iPad.

"So, big news last night, I gather," she says between sips of coffee.

"You heard already?" I pour myself some coffee and add a lot of sugar and cream. I don't usually drink coffee, but it smells really good, and maybe it will help clear my head. I've woken up feeling dazed and cranky. Not a great combo. And now I'm pissed at whoever called Mom and let the cat out of the bag, as Verna would say.

"Angela called. She assumed I knew."

"You were out last night. I fell asleep waiting for you." This is not exactly true, and I'm not sure why I'm trying to make her feel bad. It only makes me feel worse.

"I'm sorry, Harry. But we can't unring that bell, so let's move on."

I shrug and gulp down some coffee.

"How are you feeling about it? About him?"

I shrug again. "He sounds okay, I guess. Kinda boring, but okay."

She looks up and cocks an eyebrow at me. "What's going on?"

"I wanted to tell you myself. Angela shouldn't have told you. Have you read the email?"

She holds up her iPad. "Angela sent it to me, but I haven't opened it yet. I was waiting for you. If you don't want me to read it, I won't. It's not addressed to me, after all. I think Angela and Nori have been up all night talking about it."

"And they think it's a good idea to meet him when he comes back from Mexico?"

"Yup. And so do I."

"You do?"

She nods. "Aren't you curious?"

"Are you?"

"Of course. But if you don't want to meet him, that's okay too. Although I would like to thank him for his excellent genetic material."

I laugh and say, "You can read the email."

"You sure?" I nod and sit down beside her at the table as she reads.

When she gets to the end, she says, "He sounds like a nice person."

"Lucy says he sounds like me."

"In what way?"

"Cautious, careful, boring."

"She didn't actually say that, did she?"

I shake my head. "Not in so many words."

"So what do you want to do?"

"Hide."

Mom smiles. "I can understand that. It's a lot to take in. But remember our deal?"

"Yeah, I remember. No turning away from what life throws at us."

"So hiding is not an option."

"I guess not." I find the ferry schedule on my phone and say, "Could we go to Whidbey on Monday?

All of us—three sisters and their families. Hang out at Double Bluff, have a picnic."

She nods. "I could use a day off. Do you want to set it up?"

"Sure."

It's been a few years since we've been to Double Bluff, but I remember walking for miles on that beach, digging for clams, building sand castles, making s'mores over a beach fire.

"Can we stay the whole day? The ferries run really late in the summer."

"Sounds like a plan," she says.

After a flurry of phone calls, it's all set up. Alex is coming too, at Meredith's request. Could be awkward, since we haven't talked since he was at my house, but I don't say anything. At least we don't have to travel in the same car; Angela and Nori drive a hybrid SUV, and Meredith and Alex will go with them.

I try to work on another transcription, but the girl's story is so depressing—and so familiar—I can't finish it. Drugs, sex, abuse, violence, poverty. I can't handle it today. I roam the house in my pajamas, unable to concentrate on anything for more than five minutes. I try to read, but the words swim; I watch a movie, but I can't understand what the actors are saying; I put some bread in the toaster and forget to take it out; I do a load of laundry, but leave out the soap. Eventually I give up and go back to bed. I balance the spirit level on my knees and watch the bubbles move around. As I stare at it, I have an idea.

I grab my computer and start googling *Boatbuilders + Seattle*. I don't remember Ray's last name, but I figure I'll recognize it when I see it. I'm briefly excited when I find Ray's Boathouse, but it turns out to be a restaurant in Ballard. There are a lot of boatyards in Seattle, so I start calling them, asking for Ray. On my tenth try, a guy says, "Which one? Doheny or Kurtz?" and suddenly it comes back to me. I was reading *Heart of Darkness* for school when Ray and Mom were dating. I thought it was funny that his name was Kurtz.

"Kurtz," I say, and the guy yells, "Kurtz! Phone call!" The next thing I hear is Ray's voice, saying, "Ray Kurtz here."

I almost hang up, but I've gone this far, so I clear my throat and say, "This is Harriet Jacobs, Della's daughter. Um, how are you?"

"I'm fine," he says. "A bit surprised to hear from you."

"Mom and I were talking about you the other day. A friend of mine gave me one of those spirit level things, and Mom told me you had one."

"I have a few, actually."

"So I wondered if you could help me with something."

"If I can," he says.

"Could you call my mom?"

Ray laughs. "You want me to call your mom, after she broke up with me—what?—over a year ago?"

"Yes."

"I don't think so, Harriet."

"But she told me how much she liked you. How you guys were getting serious. How she didn't want to risk turning into her mother or something. How she didn't want to do anything that might mess up our lives. Not that you would have, but—"

"I get it, Harriet. But I don't think I can call her."

"Are you married or something? In a relationship?"

"No, but—"

"She'll be happy to hear from you. I promise. She misses you."

"I'll think about it. But right now, I have to get back to work."

"Thank you, Ray," I say.

"Look after that spirit level," he says. "You never know when it might come in handy."

FOURTEEN

BY THE TIME Monday morning rolls around, I am like a cat on hot bricks, as Verna would say. At sixes and sevens, on pins and needles, as jumpy as a marionette. I should never have agreed to spend a whole day with Alex and Meredith.

I throw on the dress I wore when I first met Lucy, put my hair up in a loose bun and brush on some mascara. Old Navy flip-flops complete my ensemble.

"You look relaxed," Mom says when I come downstairs. She looks pretty good herself, in white capris and a blue top that matches her eyes. "Ready to go?" she says. "Verna's been calling every five minutes. She's worried we'll miss the ferry."

I roll my eyes and grab the picnic basket from the kitchen counter. It's a potluck picnic, and I made a muffuletta, which is basically a loaf of crusty Italian bread stuffed with cheese and meat and pickled vegetables and olives. We also have iced tea and the makings for s'mores.

On the drive to Verna's, Mom says, "Maybe don't talk too much about the donor situation and the possibility of meeting your new grandmother. Verna's a bit worried."

"About what?"

"About losing you."

"That's—nuts." Then it occurs to me that maybe Mom feels the same way. I've been so focused on my own shit that I haven't considered whether my huge new extended family might make my mom feel insecure or inadequate or something. Those are not words I associate with her, but anything is possible these days.

"Are you worried too?" I ask. "'Cause you don't have to be. It's not like I've been, you know, pining for a big family all this time. It's just—"

She cuts me off. "You don't have to explain. I understand. If you want to meet all of the Ramoses eventually, you should."

She reaches out and pats my leg. "And since you ask, I've had a couple of bad moments, but I'm good. Talking to Angela and Nori has helped. And like Lucy says, you're not exactly the most reckless girl in the world. You never wanted to run away and join the circus. So I doubt that you're going to go live with the Ramoses."

When we get to Verna's, she is standing outside, wearing navy pants and a crisp white blouse and holding a shoe box. I jump out to get into the backseat, and she slides the box in after me.

"What's in the box?" I ask.

"Cinnamon buns," she says. "For the picnic."

I inhale deeply. "With cream-cheese icing?"

Mom laughs. "Those buns might get eaten on the ferry. We are going to be with four teenagers, after all. And I know this one didn't eat breakfast."

"Not my problem," Verna says. "Hands off the cinnamon buns. You hear me, Harry?"

"But I'm so hungry," I say, just to bug her. "And they smell so good. Just one for the road? Please." Verna turns around and swats me.

Mom puts on some music, and Verna immediately starts complaining—she hates Mom's music. Always has. It's one of the few things they don't agree on. Mom loves Nirvana and Pearl Jam and the Foo Fighters—all that Seattle grunge stuff. She's Dave Grohl's biggest fan. She'd marry him if she could. Verna calls it *that infernal caterwauling*. She prefers orchestral music, which bores Mom and me to tears. I put in my earbuds and listen to Marina and the Diamonds and Modest Mouse until we get to the ferry lineup. I can see Angela and Nori's SUV up ahead, but when Mom and Verna get out to say hi, I stay in the car to try and enjoy a few minutes of solitude before everything gets crazy. I'm not alone for long. Lucy knocks on the window and then jumps into the backseat. I laugh when I see what she's wearing: cargo shorts and a turquoise T-shirt. Exactly what she had on the day we met. As if there was some kind of magic in the fabrics, something that bound us to each other and protected us.

"Nice outfit," I say.

She giggles. "You too."

I look down the row of cars and see Meredith get out of the SUV. She is wearing an ankle-length purple paisley skirt, a gauzy white blouse and a wide-brimmed floppy hat. On her feet are buffalo sandals, and she is carrying a fringed leather bag.

"Whoa," I say. "She looks like she's on her way to Woodstock, not to Whidbey Island for a picnic. Where does she shop anyway?"

"Thrift shops," Lucy says. "All her stuff is secondhand. Isn't that cool? What's Woodstock?"

"The original hippie music festival, back in the day. She looks ridiculous."

"Don't be so mean, Harry," Lucy says. "She's not hurting anyone."

"You're right," I say. But I still think she looks ridiculous. Alex is out of the car now too, talking to Meredith. He is in his usual shorts and shirt—no fringed vest, thank god, or bell-bottom jeans. They appear to be arguing, if Meredith's body language—back stiff, arms crossed, shoulders elevated—is anything to go by. Lucy and I watch as she jabs Alex in the chest and he takes a step back, throwing up his hands and striding away from her and toward our car. I don't know if he's spotted us yet—I hope not—but then Lucy rolls down the window and calls him over. He is frowning and flushed when he leans down and peers into the backseat.

"Everything okay?" Lucy asks.

"Meredith's a bit on edge," he says. "Not sure why. And Churchill's asleep. Hi, Harry."

I wave weakly and am saved from speaking by the announcement that the ferry is about to load. Lucy jumps out of the car, and Alex slides into the backseat beside me. "Mind if I ride with you?" he asks. "Or are you pissed with me too? If so, it's going to be a swell day."

Once again, I'm saved from having to reply. On her way back to the SUV, Lucy executes a huge split leap—a grand jeté, I think it's called—and lands badly. I see her ankle twist and hear her yelp. She steadies herself against a nearby car to keep from falling. I start to get out of the car, but she waves me off and hobbles toward the SUV. Mom and Verna return to the car, and we drive onto the ferry. When we're on board, they head to the upper deck and I'm left alone with Alex again. No sign of Meredith or Lucy. It's only a twenty-minute ride, but I don't think I can stay silent that long, not with him so close to me. His shirtsleeves are rolled up, and I notice a scar running up his forearm and disappearing under his shirt.

"What's that from?" I ask, pointing at it.

"Fell off my bike," he says. "I was about thirteen. Some older guys were chasing me. One of them stuck a stick in my spokes. I landed on a spike in a pile of construction garbage someone had left on the boulevard. The guys took off, and some passing stranger took me to the hospital. I got thirty stitches, and when my mom finally came to pick me up and I told her what happened, all she said was *Boys will be boys.*"

The one time I had to have stitches—I stepped on some glass on the beach—Mom and Verna stayed with me every minute and never once reminded me that they had both told me, repeatedly, to wear my sandals. I got a strawberry sundae on the way home from the hospital, and we watched all my favorite movies for days afterward. And I only had four stitches.

"That's so shitty," I say.

"Yeah, well, she's right. Boys will be boys—unless they're girls." His laugh is bitter, and I want desperately to make things better for him. Someday soon we'll have to talk about Meredith, about us, but today is not the day. Today is a day for distractions. So I tell him a story, which is something Mom always did when I was upset. Mom didn't tell me stories about princesses and unicorns. She told me stories about the lives of interesting people—Georgia O'Keeffe, for instance, and Margaret Mead and Gandhi. But I want to amuse Alex, so I tell him about something that happened to Gwen and me when we were about ten.

"Gwen's family had this awesome above-ground pool, but her older brothers and their friends were always in it, and they would splash us and make giant whirlpools that sucked us under, and occasionally they would hold our heads underwater too long. No fun. One day all the brothers were out, so Gwen and I decided to use the pool, which was on a patio with big glass doors leading into the house. The second story of the house had windows above the pool, so, in our infinite wisdom, we decided to cannonball together into the pool from there." I pause for a moment. "Naked."

Alex snorts with laughter, and I continue. "So we jumped, and there was a huge *boom* as the pool exploded. Water flooded the house and flung us across the concrete patio and out into the backyard. We ended up under an apple tree, freaking out and with very sore asses from concrete burn. Gwen's mom was in the kitchen when the little tsunami hit. She was pretty cool about it, even though there were two inches of water in her house. But they never got another pool. And I bet my mom had to pay something for the damage to the house, although she never brought it up."

"Your mom is pretty great," Alex says. "You're lucky." He takes my hand in his, and I lean my head against his shoulder. We sit in silence as the ferry docks.

Before we go to the beach, we stop in Freeland for coffee. Or, in Meredith's case, herbal tea. I'm not thirsty and neither is Alex, so we stroll around the little town with Churchill and get a map of the island at the Visitor Information Center. I want to show him where we used to stay when I was a kid, in a little cabin near Useless Bay.

"Useless Bay? Really?" Alex says. "Why is it useless?"

"Probably for anchoring. I'm not sure. But my favorite beach in the world is on Useless Bay, so it's not useless to me." I point at a spot on the map. "Double Bluff Beach. That's where we're going."

"Sounds good," he says. "I could use some beach time. Not too many beaches in Missoula. Or Lubbock."

My phone rings: Mom, calling to say she and Verna are back at the car. I grab Alex's hand and hold on to it as we walk to the car. Mom sees us approach and raises an eyebrow. Verna is already buckled up and ready to go.

We follow the SUV out of Freeland and wind our way along the western edge of the island. There are a few old cottages tucked away in the trees, some monster houses right on the water and lots of ordinary places with double garages and big decks facing the ocean. We turn in to the parking lot, and the beach stretches out for miles. When I was little, I thought it went all the way to Canada.

Alex piggybacks Lucy along the beach until she finds the perfect place to sit with her back against a log. I mound some sand under her hurt foot. She has commandeered Meredith's floppy hat and amuses herself by making us pose for selfies with her. When the moms catch up, it only takes a few seconds before it's clear that we need to leave Lucy alone with Angela and Nori, who are equal parts worried and pissed off. Apparently this isn't the first time that ankle has given Lucy trouble, and she's been told repeatedly to be careful. The threat of surgery looms, according to Nori.

Mom and Verna stroll down the beach in one direction, Churchill trotting at Verna's side; Alex and Meredith head in the opposite direction, arms linked. The tide is out, and I take off my sandals and head toward the water by myself, passing some Bocci players—two tall men and a short blond woman—who are drinking beer and laughing as they saunter across the sand. The wind is whipping the woman's hair around, and her short dress flies up every now and again, revealing a pink thong. She seems unconcerned. A couple of kids are building an elaborate sand castle, with seaweed flags flying from the turrets, crab-claw ramparts and a nifty clamshell drawbridge. I stop and help them dig a channel from their moat to a nearby pool, and we stand together to watch the water fill the moat. It's the most satisfying thing I've done in a long time.

Alex and Meredith seem to have resumed their argument. I can see Alex waving his arms around; Meredith is shaking her head and hunching her bony shoulders. The wind delivers fragments to me—"I won't" and "lying" and "not right"—but I'd need to get closer to hear what they're saying. There's no way to sneak up on somebody on a wide sandy beach, so I opt for waving at Alex and walking down to the water. The next thing I know, Meredith is running up to me, with Alex close behind.

"What is your problem?" she says when she is next to me.

"My problem?"

"With me."

I glance at Alex, who is standing next to Meredith, turning a shell over and over in his hands. He looks miserable.

Suddenly I am finished with her bullshit.

"You need to stop lying to everybody," I say. "You lied to me and Lucy, you lied to our moms, and you're probably already lying to Dr. Ramos. That's just not right."

"I don't know what you're talking about," she says. "You're crazy."

"You never worked on an organic farm. You never danced in the Denver ballet. That was your brother and sister. You've got two parents in Missoula, parents who love you. Barbara and Mark. I talked to them. You ran away, and you don't even have the decency to let them know where you are."

"You talked to them? When?" Meredith yells, her face contorting.

"A while ago."

"You had no right! They're my parents! My family!"

"Then maybe you should treat them better," I say coldly. "But if it helps, they wouldn't tell me anything. They were just glad to know you were alive."

Meredith falls to her knees on the sand and buries her face in her hands. Alex stands over her, unmoving. I almost feel sorry for her, but I'm not finished. "You can't base a relationship on lies. I know that for sure. I know Alex is trans. I know you've been a good friend to him.

But that doesn't mean he can't have other friends. We like each other. A lot. You need to deal with that."

I start to walk away. Alex joins me, leaving Meredith hunched over on the sand. My heart is pounding, and I'm shaking from head to toe. I want to run as fast and as far as possible, away from my crazy sister, away from my feelings for Alex. I can see Mom in the distance, bending over to examine something on the beach—a shell, a piece of beach glass, a sand dollar. She straightens up and waves at us, her hand shading her eyes. I wave back.

And suddenly Meredith is right next to me, screaming and dancing around in a rage. If she wasn't so scary, it would almost be funny—a skinny little hippie chick freaking out. "You don't know anything," she spits at me. "You think my parents are such great people? Then why does my sister, my perfect ballerina sister, have an eating disorder? And why did they spend all their time and money and energy on her when they had two other children? Do you know what that was like? Knowing that they loved their 'real' daughter more than me? They didn't even know I was there. They didn't care when I got wasted or pregnant or locked up. As long as their precious Elizabeth was all right. Alex was all I had, and now you think you can have him? It's me he loves, and I love him. We're meant to be together. You're just a...a diversion."

And then she is on me—knocking me backward to the ground and straddling me. Alex is yelling and trying to pull her off, but she pins my arms down with her knees and starts to pummel me. I turn my face away, but she manages to land a hard punch to my jaw. The pain is astonishing. If I wasn't already on the ground, I would collapse from the shock of being hit. All I can think is, It's not like this on TV. I twist and turn, trying to avoid the blows raining down on my head and shoulders, trying to get free. Meredith continues to scream, but I can't make out the words. There is sand in my mouth, and I can hear Mom yelling at her to stop. Then it's over, as suddenly as it began. And Mom is dragging Meredith away in some sort of headlock.

"That's enough, Meredith," Mom says calmly, but she is breathing hard. She must have set a personal best running over here. "Alex is going to walk you back to the car. Angela and Nori can take you home. Make no mistake— what you did just now was assault. We could have you charged. But I'm not sure that's the best approach."

"I don't care what you do," Meredith says. She's panting, but she sounds more resigned than defiant.

"I doubt if that's true," Mom says, "but right now I need to make sure Harry's all right." She helps me to my feet, puts her arms around me and holds me close as Alex takes Meredith by the arm and leads her away. I think I'm going to puke.

"I couldn't get her off me, Mom. Neither could Alex. She was crazy strong."

"Rage will do that," Mom says. "And other things. But I can't deal with her right now. We need to get your jaw looked at. There's a hospital on the island."

It really hurts when I shake my head, but I don't tell her that. "Can we go home? I don't want to stay here any longer." I start to cry. Meredith has ruined the day—and maybe broken my jaw too. On my favorite beach.

Mom is stroking my hair and telling me it will be okay, but I'm not sure I believe her. After a few minutes we head slowly back to the car. The kids have abandoned their sand castle, and the tide is coming in. Soon it will be washed away. This seems like the saddest thing of all, and my crying escalates to sobbing.

Alex and Verna and Churchill are waiting when we get back. The SUV is gone.

"Verna said I could ride with you," Alex says. "Is that okay?"

"I guess you're going to have to," Mom says. "Unless you want to walk."

"I'm sorry, Della," he says.

"What for?"

"For what Meredith did. For not protecting Harry."

"I don't need protecting," I mumble, although clearly I do sometimes.

"What Meredith did isn't your fault, Alex," Mom says. "She's not a happy girl."

"Understatement," I mutter as I climb into the back-seat and put my head in Verna's lap.

FIFTEEN

WE ARE ON the ferry, and I am in agony. When I try to talk, it feels as if someone is slamming my face with a brick. I groan, and Mom turns around and hands me a bag of frozen peas. I'm so out of it, I didn't even know we had stopped at a store.

"This will help," she says. "We're going directly to the U Dub Medical Center. I called my friend Janet and told her what happened. She'll be waiting for us."

"You called Janet? Why?" I mumble. I sound drunk. I wish I was.

"She's an ER doctor," Mom says. "She can fast-track us. She said you should try not to talk until you've had some X-rays. And that you should take some Advil and ice your jaw."

First Lucy's ankle, and now this. Two medical emergencies in one day. Must be some kind of record. Or maybe that's what big families are like.

Mom hands me a bottle of water and a pill. I manage to swallow it, even though opening my mouth is excruciating. Alex is silent in the front seat.

Churchill is stretched out on the floor of the backseat, his massive head on Verna's feet. It must be uncomfortable, but she doesn't complain. Once in a while she'll shift around in her seat and say, "Move your head, you big galoot," but that's all. I shut my eyes and drift away from the pain, the smell of wet dog, the sound of the tires on the highway, the murmur of voices from the front seat.

It's not very busy in the ER, and soon I'm being examined by Janet, who orders X-rays and asks what happened. "Family feud," I say, and although she looks startled, she doesn't press me for more info. Mom can fill her in. Or not. I really don't care.

I must doze off, because the next thing I know I'm being wheeled to X-ray, Mom at my side. The X-ray technician says, "Whoa!" when he sees my face.

"You should see the other guy." I wince when I speak, and Mom frowns at me. Apparently, it's too soon to make a joke about it.

After the X-ray we wait some more. Finally the doctor returns with good news: no fracture, no dislocation, no broken teeth, but my face is going to be really sore and swollen for a while. No doubt there will be bruising. In other words, I'm going to look and feel like shit. I'm a bit wobbly when we walk out to the waiting room, where Verna is deep in conversation with Nancy, one of the Sunday ladies, who is waiting for a friend who has overdosed. Alex is nowhere to be seen. Verna notices me looking around and says, "He had to go to work. He wants you to text him as soon as you can."

In the car I send him a short text—**No broken bones. Heading home to sleep**—and then turn my phone off. When we get home, Mom makes me some soup while I take a shower to rinse off the sand and the sweat and the hospital stink. I start to cry when the water hits my face.

"Can you let Lucy know I'm okay?" I ask Mom as I slurp my soup out of a mug, wincing with every sip. "I don't have the energy to talk to anyone."

"Of course," Mom says. "I'll call Angela and Nori."

"I still think you should consider calling the police," Verna says. She is cutting up apples for applesauce, and she waves the knife at Mom when she speaks.

Mom sighs. "I don't think the police will give Meredith the kind of help she needs."

Verna slams the knife down on the cutting board. A chunk of apple bounces onto the floor. "I understand,

Della, but she's violent and out of control. She hurt our girl. She needs help, but she won't get any if we don't do something."

"Maybe that's true," Mom says evenly, "but it's Harry's call." She looks over at me. "Do you want me to involve the police, Harry?"

I shake my head and gasp with pain. The thought of being questioned by a cop makes me nauseous, even though I've done nothing wrong. "All I want to do is sleep and forget about it. And I don't want you guys to fight, okay?"

Verna glares at Mom, who shrugs and says, "I think we can do that."

I sleepwalk through the next few days, drinking smoothies, watching all six seasons of *Lost*, which is oddly soothing, and avoiding contact with my own "Others," including Alex. I know Mom has been in touch with Angela and Nori. I know Lucy wants to talk to me. I know I should get a grip, but I feel as lost as the survivors of Oceanic Airlines Flight 815. The only person I consider calling is Byron, although that would take more emotional energy than I currently have.

I think a lot about what Verna said to Mom about Meredith—*She needs help, but she won't get any if we don't do something*—and I wonder what I would have thought of her if I'd had to transcribe her story. Has she ever told me the truth? I still don't know. Maybe I never will. But it can't hurt to try to understand her a bit better, so I imagine I am listening to one of Mom's tapes, and I write down—on the yellow legal pad—what I hear in my head.

My name is Meredith Leatherby. I'm eighteen years old, from Missoula, Montana. I left home over a year ago and came to Seattle because I wanted to find my sperm donor and I thought he was here. My best friend, Alex, came with me. We have been friends since first grade. Alex was born female but realized when he was around eleven that he was actually a boy. I tried to keep him safe. It never seemed weird to me. His family is awful. I have two older siblings, Jackson and Elizabeth, who are twins. I found out when I was twelve that my dad, Mark, was not my biological dad, and I went nuts. I felt so betrayed. Even though I knew Mark and my mom, Barbara, loved me, I couldn't get past the lies. I started drinking and doing a lot of drugs and screwing random guys. I got pregnant a couple of times. My parents divorced because of me. So Alex and I left Missoula after high school and came to Seattle. No one here knows us, so I can make up shit about my past that's not so pathetic as my real past. It doesn't hurt anyone, but Alex doesn't like it. He wants me to be "real," whatever that means. When I found two of my half-sisters, I kept on lying—and Alex kept on being pissed about it. I could see that he really liked one of my sisters, the one called Harry, and I was jealous. For a while now, I've wanted him to be my boyfriend, but I never told him. I was afraid that he would leave me. That I wouldn't be the most important person in his life anymore. Alex was super pissed with me, and I took it out on Harry. I mean, I went nuts and beat her up. Everything just came spewing out of me—all the pain and rage and fear I'd been feeling for years. I think I may have broken her jaw before her mom dragged me off her. I'm sorry I hit Harry, and now Alex won't even talk to me. I don't know what to do.

I reread what I've written, trying to be objective. Would I have compassion for this girl if I was simply transcribing her story? Maybe. Does it make me have more compassion now? I think it would if my face didn't hurt so much.

Eventually I get bored with watching crap, and I venture out with the beagles, Kira and Nutmeg, who seem to sense that I'm not up to much. We walk decorously around the block, stopping at every tree. The next day I take out Ketch and Mayva, aka Sniffy McSnifferton. I want to see Ping-Pong, the rottie-shepherd cross, but sweet as she is, I don't think I can manage her yet. The dogs make me laugh for the first time in forever. By Sunday I am ready to go back to the salon.

I'm hoping to see Annabeth. I haven't seen her for a while, and I'm worried that she's got into Brad's clutches or something. When we get to the salon, the first thing I see is Churchill, sprawled across the loveseat. Or, more accurately, sprawled across Annabeth, who is sitting on the loveseat, a huge grin on her face.

"Whoa! What's Churchill doing here?" I ask.

"What he does best," Verna says. "Charming people." She too is grinning. "Surprise!"

"You adopted Churchill?" I stammer.

Verna nods. "I did. With your mom's blessing. We agreed that he shouldn't be in that shelter a moment longer. He's technically my dog, but I'll need some help with him. Walking him, giving him baths, a bit more training—that sort of thing. You up for that?"

In answer, I throw my arms around her and squeeze her until she squeals. Churchill barks, jumps off Annabeth's lap and bounds across the floor, almost knocking us off our feet.

"Sit!" I say, and he does. When I hold out my hand and say, "Who's a good dog?" he lifts a paw for me to shake.

"Thank you, thank you, thank you!"

Someone turns on the music, and the four of us (plus Churchill) sing along to "Hound Dog." Mom has made today's playlist, which is all songs about dogs. There's some Norah Jones, some Beatles, Neil Young, Led Zeppelin. Who knew they all loved their dogs? It's the best present she's ever given me. I dance around the salon, and Annabeth gets up to dance with me.

When Shanti walks in, she joins us, boogying to "Walking the Dog," slapping Mom's ass and exhorting her to "shake what your momma gave you."

Mom complies. Is there anything funnier than watching your mom dance? I sit down on the loveseat, and Annabeth joins me.

"Shanti's the one I asked about Brad," I tell her.

Annabeth nods. "She went out of her way to find me when one of her friends told her what a freak Brad is. Not a record producer at all. Not even a pimp. Just a real creep. I should know better than to believe a guy like him."

"How were you to know? You have an amazing voice, and one day someone important is going to hear it."

She shrugs. "I hope so. In the meantime, I'll be more careful."

"Where are you sleeping these days?" I ask.

"Parks mostly. I go to one of the shelters when I need a shower. I clean up every day at the library. Still can't get a library card though."

"Use my address." As soon as I say it, I know that I have crossed one of those invisible boundaries that Mom is always talking about. I don't care. It doesn't seem right that we can give a dog a home so easily, but this girl—this talented, funny, smart girl—has to sleep in the park.

"Thanks, Harry, but you need ID with your address on it—like a bill or something, or a driver's license."

"Oh." I get up and pull her to her feet. "Well, at least I can give you the deluxe shampoo, scalp massage and shoulder rub. And you can borrow my library card anytime."

She slides into one of the shampoo chairs and I drape a cape around her shoulders. She leans back and sighs as I wet her hair. Shanti and Mom are still dancing, and Verna is putting water in a huge bowl for Churchill.

"Stop slobbering, you big brute," she says to him. "And you two"—she gestures at Mom and Shanti—"stop your shenanigans. You're acting like teenagers."

Mom grabs Verna's hand and spins her across the room. "We should do this every week."

"Amen, sister," Shanti says as she collapses into one of the styling chairs and looks over at Annabeth and me. "But I do need my shampoo and massage."

"Soon as I'm done here," I say.

"That guy Brad is gone," Shanti says to Annabeth. "Marco chased him off." Marco is Shanti's pimp (and Rocco's dad) and a really scary dude. But useful at times, I guess.

"Thank you," Annabeth says.

"No problem," Shanti replies. "You got a phone?"

Annabeth nods.

"I'll give you my number. You can call me anytime. Come by my place. Have a meal. Meet my kids."

"Thank you," Annabeth says, and I am flooded with shame. I look over at Mom, who is tidying up a stack of towels, and think, Screw it. If Shanti can help, so can I.

When we're finished for the day, Verna and I take Churchill for a short walk so I can show her how to keep him from pulling her arm out of its socket. When we get back to the salon, I look up at the windows on the second floor and say, "I always wanted to live there, you know."

Years ago, after she first met Verna, Mom lived in a tiny space above the salon. No real kitchen and a bathroom that used to be a closet, but I always thought it could be very cool with a fresh coat of paint and some funky vintage furniture. I used to fantasize about it being my first apartment. It's been empty ever since Mom moved out. It would be perfect for Annabeth.

"I know," Verna says. "You wanted to paint sunflowers on the bathroom walls."

"Why can't we fix it up for Annabeth?" I ask. "She could work at the salon in exchange for living upstairs. I'll be back at school soon, and you know you need the help."

"Your mother wouldn't like it."

"Why? Because Annabeth is one of *her* girls? That's bullshit, and you know it. You took Mom in. Why can't we help Annabeth? She needs someone. She needs to go to school. She needs to get a library card, for god's sake!"

Verna says, "I'll think about it, Harry," and I know she will. But she won't be rushed, and I have to respect that. I also have to hope she can get Mom onside.

While I wait for Verna to make up her mind, I decide to reach out to my brothers—all three of them, including James the Mormon.

My Skype call to Ben in Australia confirms my first impression of him: he's laid back in a totally surfer-dude way but also ambitious and clever. And funny. He has two little brothers (Isaac, twelve, and Jasper, fourteen), a dad named Al, who makes wind chimes for a living, and a beekeeper mom named Nina. "Oh yeah, total hippies," he says. "Homeschooling vegans all the way. But Al's business makes a ton of money. His wind chimes are sold all over the world. They own a big chunk of land in this tiny little outback town. And he's a good dad. He's paying my tuition fees, even though he thinks when I'm an architect I'll get all up myself. He'd rather I took up pottery or the Pan flute. Nina yabbers a lot about saving the bees, but she's also a total hardass when it comes to the business. That's why they do so well. Al's the creative side of things. She's the CEO."

"Are your brothers donor kids too?" I ask.

"Nah. Nina left the States and came to Australia right after she got pregnant. She was a single mom for a while, then she met Al and the little blokes came along. Rest is history. What about you?"

I tell him about Della and Verna, and we trade Lucy stories. He has a dog, a mutt named Iggy, that he holds up to the computer. Iggy looks like a cross between a Jack Russell and something else—a dachshund maybe. I promise to send him some pictures of Churchill and the rest of my canine gang. When we say goodbye, with a promise to keep in touch, I feel as if I've made a friend.

Not so much with Adam. He makes it clear that he's only talking to me as a favor to Lucy. He doesn't want to Skype or talk on the phone. He prefers to text. I don't think he cares that Lucy has discovered a bunch more half-siblings, and he has absolutely zero interest in meeting Dr. Ramos. The only really interesting thing I find out is that he never tells anyone he's a donor child. When I ask him why, he says it's no one else's business. No wonder he moved to another city. It would be pretty hard to keep that secret with Nori and Angela and Lucy around. But I only have so much patience for communicating with my thumbs, so we don't text for long, and he doesn't suggest we do it again. Apart from the way he looks, it's hard to feel any connection to him at all, which is kind of disappointing. Maybe that will change over time, but I won't hold my breath.

I decide to be completely up front with James about why I haven't contacted him; his reply is sweet and kind.

Dear Harriet,
When I didn't hear from you, I wondered if perhaps I had come on too strong in my email. Please be assured that we will not discuss my beliefs unless you want to.

I am not ashamed of what I believe, but I do not want to alienate people either. Especially my half-siblings. I would be happy to tell you about my family and the places we have traveled, or you could tell me about your life. I will follow your lead.

Your friend,

James

And that leaves Dr. Ramos. Daniel.

Dear Dr. Ramos,

Sorry I haven't been in touch. I've been really busy with work. I have three jobs: dog walking, helping my mom out with transcriptions (long story—she's a sociologist doing research for a book) and working in my grandmother's hair salon. I am attaching a picture of myself. I think we look a lot alike.

I've never been to Mexico, but maybe now that I know I'm part Mexican, I should go sometime. Please write to me when you get a chance.

All best,

Harry

A couple of days later, he writes:

Hello, Harry,

Thank you for sending the picture. Yes, we do look a great deal alike, although you are much prettier ;-).

You look a bit like one of my nieces, Bonita, who is about your age. Meredith looks exactly like my Aunt Renata at eighteen, and Lucy, well, Lucy doesn't look like anyone in the family, but temperamentally I think she is very like my mother—passionate and kind. A whirlwind of energy. A bit on the impulsive side. Am I right?

My guess is that you are more on the cautious side, like me. Not a bad thing, overall, but not exactly flashy. But maybe I am wrong. A picture can only tell you so much. Perhaps you are as flamboyant as your grandmother too.

My work here is very satisfying and it distracts me from thoughts of Alissa. The town has never had a doctor, let alone a clinic. I plan to winter here after I find another doctor or two to help out. Rural Mexico is beautiful, but poverty-stricken. I would love to bring you all here sometime, but I'm getting ahead of myself. I must go now. I hope you write again soon.

Best regards,

Daniel

On Wednesday, I've just stepped out of the shower when the doorbell rings. Mom is home, and I can hear her open the door and say, "Come in, you fine fellow." Maybe it's Ray, although I can't imagine her calling him a fine fellow. I peek out the bathroom door and see a black blur racing down the hall toward me, nails scrabbling on the wooden floor. Churchill. Before I can shut the door, he's all over me, licking my face, which makes me yelp, and dancing around the bathroom, knocking a bottle of shampoo off the edge of the tub. I clutch my towel around me and yell at him to sit, but he's too excited, and I don't have any treats hidden in the bathroom. I shut the door and sit on the toilet until he calms down and puts his head in my lap.

"You're an idiot," I say, stroking his ears. "But a sweet idiot."

"You okay in there?" Mom asks from the hallway. "Alex borrowed Churchill from Verna, and he decided to drop by."

I grab Churchill's collar, stand up and open the door a crack. "Alex is here?" I hiss.

"In the kitchen. Why?"

"I'm not dressed. And I'm not ready for him to see me in a towel."

"Fair enough," she says. "I think you're safe to make a run for it." I can hear the laughter in her voice.

"It's not funny," I say.

"It kind of is," she replies. "I have a feeling that our hairy friend here can make anything funny."

"Hahaha. Let's go, Churchill." I race down the hall with Churchill nipping at my towel and slam the door after us once we are both in my room. Churchill immediately makes himself at home on the bed while I get dressed and brush my hair. I stare at my bruises—they're now a gross greeny-yellow—in the mirror and consider patting on some concealer. It's tempting, but I want Alex to see what Meredith did, to understand how dangerous she is. Who am I kidding? He's probably come to defend her. Or say goodbye.

Alex and Mom are sitting at the kitchen table, drinking coffee and eating banana bread. Alex flinches when he sees my face. Good. He's not looking so great himself. His halo of hair looks greasy, and he's got some zits on his forehead. The skin under his eyes is puffy and gray. His clothes are wrinkled.

"Banana bread?" Mom says to me.

"Wow, it's a regular little coffee klatch in here," I say. It comes out nastier than I meant it to, and Mom frowns at me. I sit down, grab a slice of banana bread and start to cut it up into little pieces with a knife and fork.

"Can't open my jaw too well yet," I say. "But at least I've progressed to solid food. I never want to see another smoothie."

"Duly noted," Alex says. Churchill is sitting by my chair, strings of drool hanging halfway to the floor.

Mom stands up and says, "I've got work to do. If you need anything, you know where to find me." Alex stands up as she leaves the room. I wonder who taught him his manners. They seem at odds with what little I know of his home life.

"So how are you?" he asks. "Really."

"I'm okay. Just haven't wanted to talk to anyone, you know?"

"I get that. But I needed to see you, to make sure you were all right."

"Well, now you have."

"And I thought Churchill might cheer you up." We both look over at Churchill, who is now dozing in a patch of sunlight.

"Mission accomplished," I say.

"You're making this really hard," he says.

"*I'm* making it hard? *Me?* Did I punch myself in the face? Did I lie to everybody? We both know how this happened." I push the banana bread away from me and stand up. "Maybe you should go."

Alex stays where he is, next to the sink. "You're right. I'm sorry. It's Meredith's fault, but I'm not sure she's responsible, if that makes any sense."

"Not to my face it doesn't."

"But do you understand what I'm saying?"

"Yeah—that she's kind of nuts, so she can't be held responsible for her actions. Is that about right?"

He nods. "I've known for a long time that she— well, she makes stuff up. About herself, about her family. It seemed harmless enough at first, but then she got more intense, more obsessed about her donor, started lying more, but I didn't want to admit it. She's my best friend. But that's all. She's not my girlfriend, and I really didn't know she wanted to be. You have to believe me.

But she'd do anything for me. And now I have to do something for her."

Here it comes, I think. He's going to say goodbye. I sit down and start folding a napkin into a fan. He sits too and reaches over to still my hands.

"We need to get her some help," he says.

"We?"

"I'm not sure where to start. I thought maybe your mom might have some ideas."

I pull my hands away. So this is still about Meredith, not about us. I wonder if it will ever be about us. But if Meredith never gets help, we won't stand a chance at all. I can see that now.

I get Mom from her office, and when I tell her what Alex wants, she switches into professional mode, asking questions, making notes.

"I know Meredith stayed with Angela and Nori for a night or so after the incident at the beach," she says. "She was in rough shape. Where is she now?" This is news to me, that Lucy's family gave Meredith shelter after what she did to me. It pisses me off.

"At our place. In her room, in bed," Alex says. "She only gets up to go to the bathroom. I don't think she's eating, and she won't talk to me. She's been fired from both of her jobs. I'm going to have to get a second job, I guess. Give up the animal-shelter stuff." He looks over at Churchill, who is running in his sleep and barking softly.

"You can't do that," I say. "You love working at the shelter. The dogs need you."

"Not as much as Meredith does."

"This has gone beyond your ability to look after her, Alex," Mom says. "She needs professional help. Let me make a few calls, but first of all, do you think she's suicidal?"

Alex flinches. "I don't know. She could be. She won't talk to me."

"Has she ever attempted suicide?"

"Not that I know of," he says. "Unless you count drinking until she blacks out."

"I do," Mom says, "if it goes hand in hand with other symptoms. And where are her parents?"

"Missoula."

"How would you feel about calling them?"

Alex puts his head in his hands and shudders. "I promised her I wouldn't. She hates them."

"I could call them again," I say.

"Again?" Mom says, eyebrows raised. "You've called them before? I'm not even going to ask how you tracked them down."

"It wasn't that hard. I have excellent research skills, you know. Learned from a master." I smile at her, but she doesn't smile back.

"That's a real invasion of privacy, Harry. Theirs and Meredith's," Mom says sternly. "You should know better."

"I probably shouldn't have called, okay? I know that. But how else was I going to find out whether all that stuff Meredith told us—the dance company in Denver, the shelter in Boise, the organic farm—was true? I told them she was in Seattle with Alex. That's all."

"And what did they tell you?"

"Not much. They were glad to hear she was okay, and they told me to call again if anything was wrong."

Mom turns to Alex. "What do you think? Will they help her now?"

He nods. "Yeah, they'll help. She won't like it though."

"Probably not," Mom says, "but we have to start somewhere."

Within the hour, the three of us are huddled around my laptop at the kitchen table, Skyping with Barbara and Mark, who are in what looks like a breakfast nook. After the introductions are made, Mom gives them a brief, almost clinical update. They are horrified when they hear that Meredith attacked me, but apparently it's not an isolated incident. She was arrested in Missoula for beating up a girl who bullied Alex. Put her in the hospital. She'd gotten off with community service, but she left Missoula the day after her sentencing.

"I don't know Meredith that well," Mom says, "but I know this shouldn't be Alex's responsibility."

Mark and Barbara nod. "We'll come and get her. Bring her back home and try to get her some help."

"You should know the kids found their donor a while ago."

Alex finally speaks up. "That day on the beach, I told her it was wrong to lie to everyone. She freaked out and took it out on Harriet."

Barbara looks puzzled, so I fill in the blanks. "Alex and I were spending time together. She's threatened by our relationship, I guess."

"Still no excuse for violence," Mom says.

Barbara and Mark nod. "We're so sorry, Harriet," Barb says.

I should say, *It's not your fault*, but I'm not feeling that generous. Nature, nurture—who really knows? "I'm kind of beat," I say instead. "Think I need a nap and a pain-killer. That okay?"

Mom nods. Alex and Churchill follow me into the living room, where I lie down on the couch and close my eyes. Churchill drapes himself across my legs and feet, like a heavy hairy afghan.

Alex perches on the arm of the couch near my feet. "You think we might have a chance?" he asks.

"Of what?"

"You know what. Of being a couple."

"Maybe. If you weren't—" I stop myself before I say something cruel. He looks so beaten down, and I haven't got any fight left in me.

"Weren't what? A girl? A wuss?"

"I didn't say that. I know it's complicated. I know you love Meredith. I know you'll do anything for her. But I don't know where I fit in. *If* I fit in. And then there's all the trans stuff. Not like that's gonna be a walk in the park."

His shoulders droop. "I want to figure it out, Harry. I do. Can we just put things on hold until Barbara and Mark come? Until I know Meredith's taken care of?"

"Do you think she'll go with them?"

"Not without a fight," he says.

SIXTEEN

I DON'T WANT to see Meredith again, but she wants to see me. "To apologize," Alex says. That's hard to imagine, but I decide to get over myself. Besides, I'm curious. Will she be in a straitjacket or shackled to the bed? Part of me hopes so. The mean part. The part I never knew I had.

Barbara and Mark flew out from Missoula the day after we Skyped. They had Meredith admitted to the hospital the same day. Apparently she was dehydrated and hallucinating and too weak to argue with them.

"She's in a regular ward," Alex says as we drive to the hospital a few days later. "Barbara and Mark didn't want her in the psych ward. Too stigmatizing."

"And she hasn't tried to escape?"

"Not yet," Alex says. "I hate to say it, but I think she likes the attention. Especially from her parents."

"Sounds like she's doing what her sister did—starving herself and acting nuts."

"Liz was hospitalized a couple of times, but she never acted nuts. Not that I know of anyway. She collapsed when she was dancing, and it turned out she was living on a diet of cottage cheese and iceberg lettuce."

"Like that's not nuts."

"You know what I mean. No outbursts, no drugs, no violence."

"And what's Jackson like?"

"Jackson's cool. Bit of a zealot about organic food but otherwise harmless."

"Do they know what's going on with Meredith?"

"No idea."

We roll up to the hospital and find a place to park.

"Ready?" Alex says, taking my hand.

"Let's do it," I say.

We ride up to the ward in silence. On our way to Meredith's room, an older man shuffles past us, head down, muttering to himself. A nurse in pink scrubs calls after him, "Tea in the lounge in fifteen minutes, Gordon."

The man looks up and flashes us a radiant smile. "Will there be chocolate biscuits?" he says. He has an English accent and broken teeth.

"Don't know, mate," Alex says. "Shall I ask?"

"That would be most kind," the man says as he shuffles away.

We check in at the nurses' station and request the chocolate biscuits for Gordon before we head down the hall to Meredith's room.

"Barbara and Mark are paying for a private room," Alex says. "It's not bad, considering."

He opens the door and stands aside to let me in. Meredith is sitting up in bed. Her parents are in chairs pulled up on either side of her. Barbara is holding her hand, but when we come in, she stands up and gives me a hug.

"We weren't sure you'd come, were we, Merry?"

Meredith blinks very slowly and says "Hi" in a croaky voice. She looks awful: all gray skin stretched over jutting bones. You could lacerate yourself on her collarbones. Her hair is flattened to her skull. Her lips are cracked. An IV line trails from one scrawny arm. "Thanks for coming."

Barbara offers me her chair, but I shake my head. Even though Meredith looks too weak to hurt me, you never know. I know that mental instability can make people violent, and I don't trust Meredith. Although she looks pretty well medicated. I actually feel sorry for her, which surprises me.

"Your face okay?" She slurs her words a bit.

I lift my hand to my jaw. "Yeah, it is now."

"I'm sorry," she says. "I shouldn't have done that."

"You think?"

"I was under so much pressure. Meeting you and Lucy. Finding Daniel. Thinking I was losing Alex. I wanted everything to be perfect. I wanted to be perfect."

"I get that, but you shouldn't have lied. Not to me, not to Lucy, not to Daniel." I can hear Barbara's intake of breath, but I don't care. Meredith asked me here. She must have known I wouldn't be all that thrilled to see her.

She bows her head, and a tear trickles down her face and onto the front of her hospital gown. Crocodile tears? I'm not sure. Seeing Meredith like this is a shock. Maybe Alex is right—maybe Meredith can't be held responsible for her behavior. But I still want her to be.

"My parents want me to go back to Missoula," Meredith says through her tears. "See a therapist. Work some shit out. Get healthy again."

"That's good," I say.

"I want Alex to come back with me, but he won't. He says his life is here now. That he can't go back, not even for me."

I don't know what to say. I want to give a fist pump and throw my arms around Alex, but Mom taught me not to gloat. Not noticeably anyway. And I know it's not that simple.

"So you won," Meredith said.

"Won what?" I say.

"This round."

"Jesus, Meredith, this isn't a boxing match, and I'm not some—trophy." Alex speaks for the first time since we came into the room. "Missoula was hell for me.

You know that. I have a life here, and yeah, I hope that life includes Harry. I'll always be your friend. That will never change. But I can't go back there."

Meredith nods. "Look at this, Harriet," she says. She pulls down the shoulder of her gown to reveal a tattoo of what looks like a couple of mountain peaks— maybe one of them is Mount Jumbo. "Meredith and Alex," she says. I look more closely and see that the peaks are an uppercase *M*. Upside down, between the peaks, is an uppercase *A*. Tears sting my eyes as I back away from her.

She stretches her chapped lips into one of her weird smiles. "Some things are forever, right, Alex?" Then she turns her head away from us and closes her eyes.

"I think that's enough for now," Mark says. He ushers us out to the hallway.

"I'm sorry, Mr. Leatherby," Alex says. "I didn't mean to upset her."

Mark sighs and pats Alex on the back. "Hard not to these days, son. She's pretty far down the rabbit hole. It'll take a while to get her medication adjusted. Some of the stuff she says—well, you have no idea. Or maybe you do. But the doctor says we have to let her air her grievances, and believe me, she has a lot of them. But thanks for coming. And Harry? Please thank your mom again for us—she was a huge help."

⁓

"Are you sure you don't want to go with her?" I say as we are driving back to my place.

Alex stares out the window and rubs his hands up and down his thighs.

"Didn't you hear what I said back there? I can't go with her," he croaks, and I realize he is near tears. "You know that. Not even for Meredith."

"Okay," I say. "I get it."

He turns toward me and says, "I doubt if you do." He curls away from me and leans his head against the window.

We drive in silence for a few miles and then he says, "I'll have to start job hunting. The rent won't pay itself. Barbara and Mark paid Meredith's share for next month, but I'm on my own after that. I'll probably have to move."

When we get to my house, Mom is on the phone in her office, and there is a pie on the kitchen counter. A heart is cut out of the pastry on the top—Verna's signature.

"Want some?" I ask, and Alex nods. I get three plates and pull the ice cream out of the freezer. Verna is a genius. If anything can make us feel better today, it's pie.

"What's the date today?" Alex asks as I cut the pie.

When I tell him, he says, "Monday is my mom's birthday."

"Will you call her?" I remember the venom in her rasping voice, and I want to tell him not to call. She doesn't deserve him.

"I always do. She usually hangs up on me when I tell her I'm still a boy, but I keep trying. Glutton for punishment, I guess."

I nod and take a bite of pie. Strawberry-rhubarb. Heaven.

"How is Meredith?" Mom asks when she joins us.

"Okay, I guess," Alex says. "Skinny." He leans back in his chair and closes his eyes. The shadows under them look like the bruises I had on my jaw. Caused by the same person. "Her parents want to take her back to Montana. I think she's going to go."

Mom nods. "That's good, Alex."

"She really wanted you all to like her," Alex says. "That's why she made stuff up—to impress you. To create a new family for herself."

"I understand," Mom says. "Families can be— challenging."

"Is yours?" Alex asks.

"Absolutely," Mom says.

"Mom doesn't talk to her parents, and I've never met them," I say. "They're raging alcoholics. She ran away from home when she was a bit younger than I am."

"But you still have happy lives," Alex says.

"Absolutely," Mom says again.

Alex says nothing. I wonder if he's thinking of his own awful family.

"And now we have to figure out how to support Meredith too," Mom says. "Because she's family now. Right, Harry?"

I busy myself with cutting another piece of pie. I'm sure Mom registers my lack of response. But how can she expect me to feel good about helping someone who punched me in the face? Has she forgotten already? Or has she gone into youth-worker mode, making an assessment, accessing resources, solving problems?

"We can Skype her once she's settled," Alex says. "And maybe we could take a road trip to see her sometime."

"I'm sure Verna will want to give her that new afghan to take back to Missoula," Mom says. "To remind her of us."

"Better make sure the wool is spun by fair-trade workers from the fleece of free-range sheep," I mutter.

I don't mean to say it out loud, but the effect is predictably dramatic. Mom frowns at me and says, "It never hurts to be kind, Harry," and Alex gets up and leaves.

I keep busy with the dogs and the salon, trying to ignore the fact that Alex hasn't called since the day we went to the hospital. At least Lucy's still talking to me. She's busy, too, preparing her Baby Ballet class for an end-of-summer recital. She's had to cancel her own solo—her ankle is still wonky. When we meet for coffee one afternoon, she has a compression bandage around her ankle and she's wearing sturdy brown sandals with Velcro fastenings.

"Like my old-lady sandals?" she says. "No heels, no flip-flops. Doctor's orders."

"I like them," I say. "You look very—"

"Dorky?"

"I was going to say outdoorsy, but dorky works too."

She takes a sip of her iced tea and looks at me over the rim of her glass. "I went to visit Meredith the other day."

"Oh yeah. How was she?"

"Okay, I guess. She's getting out soon."

"That's good."

"Why don't you like her, Harry? Apart from the whole thing on the beach. Is it because of Alex?"

"Why would it be about Alex?"

"Because she's in love with him. And you like him. And he's, you know, torn."

I roll my eyes. "Oh please. We're not characters in a teen novel."

"No, but I'm right, aren't I?"

"I guess. But it's more than that. Meredith never tells the truth about anything. She's…not exactly fake, but kind of a fantasy version of herself. I don't trust her."

"I get that," Lucy says, "but it makes me sad that my sisters don't like each other. I mean, we all have fantasies.

Mine was that we would be close. *Sisterhood of the Traveling Pants* close. And now I feel like I'm in the middle. I know Meredith's not perfect, but neither are you. Or me." She picks up a napkin and blows her nose loudly.

I resist saying that the girls in *Sisterhood of the Traveling Pants* weren't actually sisters. Instead I say, "I'm sorry. It's just hard to like someone who has, you know, attacked you."

"I get that," Lucy says. "But it still makes me sad." She stands and starts to gather up our dirty dishes. I take them from her and put them in a gray plastic bin near the café's kitchen. I look around for Nate, but he's nowhere in sight. Maybe he got his big break and is in Hollywood, making a movie. Or maybe he's out back, smoking and running lines.

I walk Lucy back to the dance studio and watch her take the tiny ballerinas through their routine. She is patient and kind, even when one little girl has a meltdown and refuses to get up off the floor. I envy that little girl. It's what I've felt like doing every day since Alex walked out the door. When I catch Lucy's eye and wave goodbye, she blows me a kiss, and the little girls mimic her, as if it's all part of their routine. Maybe it is, but it still feels good.

Verna comes over to talk about Annabeth a couple of days later. Mom, as predicted, doesn't take it well.

"Whose idea was this?" she says, glaring at me.

Before I can speak, Verna says, "Ours. Harry's and mine. We've all gotten to know Annabeth over the years—"

"And some of what you know is because of my research," Mom says. "That information is privileged, Harry. This is a complete violation of ethics. You could put my whole study in jeopardy."

"How so?" Verna says. "Harry hasn't used any of that information unethically, nor will she. I don't see a case study when I look at Annabeth. I see a young woman who could use my help. Our help."

"Don't you think I see that too?" Mom says. Her face is flushed, and her hands are clenched in her lap.

"Of course you do," Verna replies. "You just aren't in a position to do much about it. I am."

"I am doing something," Mom says. "My work."

"I'm not saying your work doesn't help, Della, but I want to do more. And Harry does too."

"Harry doesn't know the first thing about it. The commitment. The sacrifices. The disappointment."

"And you do?" I ask. "We wouldn't be sitting here now if Verna hadn't taken you in. I probably wouldn't even exist. You've always told me that. How can you deny Annabeth the same thing? Seems to me you've been on the receiving end, but the rest of it's all theoretical now. Academic. What is it you always say? *Research can't replace experience.* So let this be *my* experience."

"That's not fair, Harry, and you know it. I burned out as a front-line worker, and being an academic has given me—us—lots of things we wouldn't have had otherwise. This house, for instance. Your straight teeth. Vacations. Security. A decent car. So don't talk to me about research and experience."

She glares at me, but I stand my ground. "That doesn't mean we can't still help someone. Annabeth is awesome. She deserves a break. This is important, Mom. You know it is."

"She could be another success story," Verna says. "Like you, Della."

Mom nods slowly, and in that moment I see Annabeth's life opening up like a peony bud on a warm June day.

"Does she know anything about this?" Mom asks.

"Of course not," Verna says. "And she won't until we can get her over here and tell her together. In the meantime, Harry has volunteered to get the apartment in shape."

"You sure about this, Harry?" Mom asks.

"Absolutely," I say.

SEVENTEEN

THE NEXT DAY, when Annabeth comes to the salon, I invite her home for dinner. She seems puzzled but happy to come. I wait to tell her about the apartment and the job at the salon until we are sitting at the table on the back patio with Verna and Mom, drinking lemonade and watching Churchill chase his own tail. At first she can't stop crying, and she keeps looking from one of us to the other and saying, "Are you sure? Are you sure?"

Verna pats her hand and says, "Yes, honey, we're sure," and Annabeth cries some more. Eventually Mom says, "Anyone else hungry? I'm starving. Hope you like salmon burgers, Annabeth. And chocolate cake. Harry's specialty."

Annabeth nods and sniffles. "Can I help with anything?" she asks.

"Nope," Mom says. "Harry and I have got it covered. You just relax and choose some colors for your new place."

She slides a book of color samples across the table to Annabeth, whose eyes widen. "I get to choose?"

"Of course you do," Verna says. "It's only two rooms, if you count the bathroom. But you don't have to paint every wall the same color, you know."

Annabeth seems dazed. "I don't?" She fans out the colors. "I've never chosen a room color. I don't know where to start."

"Start with what you love," Verna says.

"Yellow. Not bright yellow. Something soft."

Verna reaches over and thumbs through the colors. "How about this one? Fun in the Sun? Or Sunshine on the Bay. That's appropriate, don't you think?"

After dinner we clean up the dishes and then sit in the living room with the color samples on the coffee table in front of us. Once Annabeth has chosen colors for all the rooms, Verna leaves and Mom goes to her room to read.

I don't want Annabeth to go back to the park or wherever she's sleeping.

"You could stay here," I say. "Until the apartment's ready."

She shakes her head. "I've been sleeping at Shanti's. On the couch. She's been real good to me. I can't just disappear. And I want to tell her the good news face-to-face. But I'll be safe, I promise. I've been helping out with the kids, and I want to keep doing that. I'll be fine. Better than fine."

"Okay," I say as I hug her goodbye. "Call if you need me."

"I will. And thanks again. You can't know what this means to me. To have friends and a place to live." She starts to tear up again.

"Enough with the happy tears," I say.

I haven't been in the apartment above the salon for years, and it's smaller and dingier than I remember. And piled with boxes. Some of them are full of ancient salon supplies. Some are stuffed with Mom's old university papers. A few hold Verna's old clothes. I snag a yellow polka-dot shirt with only one tiny bleach spot on it. A box of books turns out to be mostly sociology texts. I send Mom pictures of all her stuff and she texts back **Turf it**. I drag the box downstairs to the Dumpster and toss it in.

When I've gotten rid of all the junk, I start cleaning. Annabeth has offered to help, but I don't want her to see the place until it's clean and painted and furnished. Light floods in through the windows after I scour them with soap and vinegar and polish them with crumpled-up newspaper. The floor has the same lino as the salon but much less faded, and I scrub it until it almost gleams. Ditto for the shower stall and sink and toilet.

I've been haunting thrift shops and have found a dresser, a wooden coat rack, a tiny kitchen table and chairs, a bed frame and a nightstand. I pay for everything except the new mattress, which Mom is buying. The apartment-size fridge and stove still work. Verna has an old overstuffed chair that she wants Annabeth to have. That's about all that will fit in the room.

Lucy helps me paint. Sunshine on the Bay in the main room, Blue Angel in the bathroom. Cloud White trim. Something called Rose Parade for the table and chairs. When the paint is dry, we haul the rest of the furniture up the stairs and arrange it in the little room, angling the big blue corduroy chair so Annabeth will be able to look out the window at the sky. Lucy has brought new towels from Nori and Angela—green as a bamboo shoot. The mattress arrives, and Lucy and I make up the bed with linens Mom has kept since my sunflower phase when I was about six. A white vase sits on the table, filled with flowers cut from Nori's garden.

"I always wanted to live here, you know," I say to Lucy, who is curled up in the big chair.

"It's adorable," Lucy says. "Annabeth is gonna love it."

The big reveal takes place on Saturday afternoon. It's crowded in the little room—Shanti has brought her kids; Nori and Angela are there too. There's champagne (soda for the little kids) and cupcakes from Cupcake Royale. Verna brings Annabeth up the stairs, a pink scarf tied over her eyes, and when Annabeth takes off the blindfold, I'm afraid she's going to faint. Shanti puts her arm around her, grins and says, "Get a grip, girl."

"No crying," I yell, but everyone does anyway.

"Happy tears," Annabeth whispers in my ear when she hugs me. "Happy tears."

And I am crying too. Mostly with happiness, but also because I haven't heard from Alex since the day he walked out of my house, and I miss him.

A few days after Annabeth moves into the apartment, the phone rings just as I'm falling asleep. I squint at the call display. Alex.

"Did I wake you up?" he says.

"Sort of. What's up?"

"I have to tell you something."

"Okay." I'm wide awake now, sure he's going to tell me he's decided to go to Missoula with Meredith.

"You're not going to like it, but I couldn't not tell you, even though Meredith would flip out if she knew I called you."

"Spit it out."

"When Meredith got out of the hospital, she asked her parents if she could have a few days with me, at our place, to sort out some stuff. Say goodbye. She told them they needed to trust her and give her some space before she goes back to Missoula. They agreed. Mark's already gone back. He had to work. Her mom's still at a hotel."

"So what won't I like?"

"Meredith's decided to take the bus down to Mexico and see Daniel. She's convinced he's going to be murdered by a drug cartel before she has a chance to meet him. Which is not as crazy as it sounds. He's in this tiny village in Durango. The drug cartels kill visitors all the time. I can't let her go there by herself, Harry. I just can't. No matter how much I care about you, if anything happened to her…"

"Stop. I get it." And I do, even though what he's saying makes me feel faint.

"So you understand?" He sounds so hopeful it breaks my heart.

"Yup. Sort of." What I understand is that I can't do anything about their relationship. I can't make him stop caring about her. I can't make her less needy. All I can do is be myself, level-headed Harriet.

"We're going to call Barbara once we're on the road," Alex says. "And I'll be back soon, Harry."

"If the drug cartels don't murder you first."

"That's not funny."

"Sorry. What do you want me to say? That I think it's a great idea? I don't. And I don't have to like it."

"I know. I'm sorry."

"Me too." I can't think of anything more to say, other than "Be safe," which I whisper before I hang up.

And now the tears come, drenching my pillowcase. I'm pretty sure I break the fifteen-minute rule.

Lucy calls the next morning. All I can hear when I pick up are sobs and the occasional hysterical hiccup.

"Lucy, calm down. Breathe. What's wrong?"

"I'm not supposed to tell you," she manages to say.

"Not supposed to tell me what?" I sit up in bed and turn on the light.

"That they're leaving."

"It's okay, Lucy. I already know. Alex told me."

"But it's terrible. Right? Barbara and Mark are going to be so upset. I can't even imagine doing something like that to my moms."

"I agree, but I don't think Meredith sees it that way. And I bet Barbara won't be all that surprised."

"Should we call her?" Lucy asks.

"Who, Barbara? No," I say slowly. "It's between her and Meredith."

"But she'll be so worried."

I sigh. "Yeah. I know. But Alex says they're going to call her when they're on the road. She might not even realize they're gone until then."

Lucy blows her nose loudly. "Meredith thinks you hate her," she says.

"I don't hate her. I just don't trust her."

"But she's your *sister*," Lucy says, her voice rising on the word. "And she's not okay. She got discharged from the hospital, but she's so skinny."

"Maybe eating Mexican food will fatten her up."

"Why are you being like that?" Lucy asks.

"Like what?"

"Hard. Mean."

"I'm not trying to be mean. I'm trying to be..."

"Sensible," Lucy says. "I know." It definitely doesn't sound like a compliment this time. She hangs up, and I toss my phone onto the duvet and burrow under the covers. My last thought before I go back to sleep is, I can't wait to talk to Gwen.

EIGHTEEN

TWO WEEKS AFTER school starts, I'm sitting
with Gwen at Café Allegro, waiting for Lucy to finish
dance class and join us. Nate has made us his "signature" drink, which he calls The Norton after his favorite
actor. As far as I can tell, it's just an iced chai latte, but
it's still good.

"He's cute," Gwen says after Nate tells us about his
latest role (Action, in a revival of *West Side Story*). "And
he likes you."

"That's what Lucy says, but I think he's just a chronic
flirt."

"So why didn't he offer *me* a ticket to his show?"
Gwen says. "Aren't I hot enough?" She pretend-pouts
and sticks out her boobs. I burst out laughing. Gwen
looks ridiculously good—she's in a short black-and-
white, pleat-skirted designer dress she bought in Paris

with her new stepmom. "I'm wearing Isabel Marant," she says, "but I guess your boy Nate prefers whatever you're calling your look."

"It's my new line. I call it 'Clean-Laundry Couture.' Who's Isabel Marant?" I ask.

Gwen rolls her eyes. "Like you care."

I laugh again. She looks amazing, but out of place in the funky café. "So how was Dominique?"

"Nice, I guess. All she does is shop and eat the tiny, perfect low-carb meals their chef prepares for her. Oh yeah, and go to Pilates. But Dad's happy. Not that I saw him very much. Too busy making money for Dominique and me to spend. And for alimony and child support."

I reach over and take her hand. "I'm glad you're back. Really glad. It's been insane here."

"Sounds like it. You've, like, lived a whole huge life while I've been away. All the time I was in France, I imagined how bored and lonely you must be without me." She snorts. "Last time I make that mistake."

"Yeah, I was so bored I found five half-siblings, my donor and a trans boyfriend."

"So Alex is your boyfriend? Even though he took off for Mexico with your crazy half-sister?"

"Well, maybe not boyfriend. Not yet. But he says he's definitely coming back, so we'll see. Apparently Daniel wasn't all that thrilled when they turned up unannounced. He made Meredith call Barbara so he could discuss the situation with her. Meredith might stay and work at the clinic for a while. Running the office or something. Alex says she's a different person in Mexico. Focused. Happy. He thinks it's because Daniel expects her to contribute something. Help out. Get involved."

"So that's good, right? For you and Alex?"

"I hope so. But I'm not holding my breath. Even if he comes back, he might get a call one day from Meredith and be gone again. And there's the whole trans thing. It's not exactly simple."

"Is it ever?" Gwen sighs. "Dominique introduced me to some of her friends in Paris. Her guy friends. They're only a few years older than Zach, but they're so—"

"French?"

"Sophisticated. Wine and steak frites, not beer and burgers and fries. And their clothes? Omigod, Harry! Pants that fit. Handmade shoes. Cartier watches. I'm not sure I can go back to baggy jeans and T-shirts."

"Give it a few weeks," I say. "And Zach's not that bad. He's just not French. Or twenty-two. You're experiencing culture shock. You'll get over it."

"So what about you and Byron? Zach says he'll be here soon. Does he know about Alex?"

"Yeah. But not that he's trans. That's not my story to tell."

"You told me," she says.

"But I asked Alex first if it was okay."

"I get it. So I shouldn't go around telling everyone at school that your new guy used to be a girl named Danielle?"

"Not if you want to live to shop another day."

The door of the café opens and Lucy barrels in, coming to a screeching halt in front of us. "Omigod, are you wearing Isabel Marant?" she squeals. When Gwen nods, Lucy drops her bag on the floor, pulls her chair close to Gwen's and says, "Where did you get it?"

Gwen laughs. "I'm Gwen, by the way. You must be Lucy. And I got it in Paris."

"I'm going to dance in Paris one day," Lucy announces. "And shop."

"You'll love it," Gwen says, "as long as you have lots of money. And I mean *lots*. Lucky for me, my dad is loaded. And he feels guilty, so it's a win-win for me."

I know she doesn't really mean it. No closet full of designer clothing can make up for the fact that her dad is gone and her mom is depressed and they had to sell their house and move into an apartment.

As I half-listen to Lucy and Gwen discuss the latest Paris runway fashions, I think about what it will be like to see Byron again. We've been talking on the phone a lot. He knows about Alex; I know about a girl named Martha that he hooked up with in New York. He's coming back for a lot of reasons, he tells me—not just for me. He says he misses the ocean and the air and Zach and the pizza at Delancey and the basketball program at our school and the Space Needle.

But you've got the Empire State Building and the Statue of Liberty, I said the last time we talked. *And pizza.*

Not the same, he said. *Take my word for it. I'm not ready for New York. Maybe I'll come back here for college, but for now I need the rain and the green and my friends.*

As I take a sip of my Norton, I realize that Gwen and Lucy have stopped talking and seem to be waiting for me to speak.

"Did I miss something?" I ask. "Other than whether mink is making a comeback in couture?"

"I asked you if you wanted to come for dinner tonight," Lucy says. "You and Gwen. Angela and Nori are cool with it. They're going to call your mom. We'll make pizza on the barbecue. Celebrate the end of summer."

"I don't think I can. I'm supposed to have dinner with Annabeth and Verna."

"They can come too," Lucy says, her fingers flying over her phone. "The moms won't mind. Please, Harry."

"You see what I have to put up with," I say to Gwen. "Little sisters are such a pain." I reach out and ruffle Lucy's hair. She slaps at my hand.

"I can see that," Gwen replies. I don't think I'm imagining that she sounds a bit wistful. It's not like she can talk to her brothers about designer fashion.

Lucy's phone pings, and she reads the message. "Angela says that's fine. Harry, can you let Annabeth and Verna know? Then we have to pick up some stuff for the pizza. And your mom needs to get some wine, but Angela will text her."

We get up and clear our dishes. Nate reminds me to come in next week and pick up my ticket for his show.

As we leave the café, Gwen slings her arm around my shoulders. Lucy bounces along in front of us.

"I'm glad you're back," I say. "I missed you."

"And I'm sorry I missed all the drama. Lucy's great, and I can't wait to meet Alex and see Byron again. It's like a whole love triangle. So romantic."

"It's not really a triangle," I say. "More like a quadrangle. And it's not very romantic to get punched in the face, let me tell you."

"I hear you," Gwen says. "But it's still an improvement over your usual boring existence. Am I right, Lucy?"

Lucy giggles. "Have you seen what Alex gave her?"

Gwen pokes me. "No, I haven't. Hope it wasn't roses. Harry hates roses."

"Only the kind that come in a box," I protest. "And he didn't give me roses. He gave me a spirit level."

Gwen stops walking. "He gave you a what?"

"A carpenter's level. An old one. It's pretty cool."

"So he gave you, like, an old tool?"

"Yup."

And suddenly we're all laughing so hard we can't speak, and people are stepping around us on the sidewalk and smiling, because really, who can be mad at us? We're sisters—by blood or not, it doesn't matter. It's our prerogative to disrupt the world with our lunacy. I remember what Meredith said when I first met her, about wanting to share her journey with Lucy and me, and I wonder if that will ever happen. I emailed her after Alex told me that Daniel wasn't exactly thrilled to see them. I'm not sure why. Maybe it was because of something Annabeth said when we were at the salon one day. I'd been telling her about Meredith, and she stopped sweeping and said, *Don't you think everyone deserves a second chance?* She didn't sound judgmental at all—she never does—just curious, as if it was a question she asked herself all the time.

So I wrote to Meredith, very cautiously, asking her to tell me about Mexico. Eventually, she wrote back. We've exchanged a few emails since then. We don't talk about Alex or Daniel. She tells me stories about the kids in the village and how her Spanish is getting better every day. I tell her about finding Annabeth a vocal coach. And now, as I walk down the street with Gwen and Lucy, I wonder what it would be like if Meredith was here with us, laughing like a loon and looking forward to a family dinner. Maybe one day she will be.

ACKNOWLEDGMENTS

Robin Stevenson, Kirsten Larmon and Monique Polak read an early version of *Spirit Level* and provided me with thought-provoking, insightful and often contradictory comments.

Cameron Duder and Leo Forbes Knox helped me to understand what it means to be transgender; Tim Prekaski shared his encyclopedic knowledge of Seattle; the divinely talented Claire Butterfield was my musical director.

Allison Cooper wrote the moving article that is quoted on page 126.

Lu Bittner and the whole Bittner/Silver clan of Bella Coola and Hawaii inspired me to include a transgender character in the story.

Jen Cameron and Maggie de Vries were unfailingly supportive and encouraging, even when I pronounced the book total garbage. My children, Fiona and Christian, continue to be my biggest fans and a source of much amusement and joy.

The Orca Pod was, as always, a delight to work with, as was the Orca Kennel—Ketch, Mayva, Kira and Nutmeg.

Family dogs Ping-Pong, Scout, Kingsley and Cocoa (RIP) reminded me that sleeping in the sunshine and chasing your own tail are perfectly acceptable life goals.

The BC Arts Council's generous support made it possible for me to meet my self-imposed deadlines.

And finally, Barbara Pulling, editor extraordinaire, guided me through the dark woods of numerous revisions. Without her, this book might well have been total garbage.

Thank you, one and all.

SARAH N. HARVEY is the author of numerous
books for children and teens. She lives in Victoria, British
Columbia, where she works as a children's-book editor.
For more information, go to www.sarahnharvey.com.